"Where is my brother?"

Ethan's question brought Kelly's attention to him. Nico stood beside him, guarding him. It seemed as though the dog still considered him to be someone worth protecting.

I agree.

Franko said, "That's what the dog will tell us." He shoved her. "Now go."

Under armed guard, they walked to the front door. Part of Kelly wondered if her dad had managed to call the cops. Would there be a swarm of officers outside?

She didn't want to be in a hostage situation.

"Bring whatever you need to search for Brett. Because your dog is the one that's going to find him."

At the front door, she glanced back at Franko. "Who told you that?"

"Does it matter? I know the mutt can do it."

He shoved her and she stumbled out the front door into Ethan. He caught her, but she had to pull away so these guys didn't think he could be used as leverage against her.

They had to believe he was just another innocent bystander as far as she was concerned.

Lisa Phillips is a British-born, tea-drinking, guitar-playing wife and mom of two. She and her husband lead worship together at their local church. Lisa pens high-stakes stories of mayhem and disaster where you can find made-for-each-other love that always ends in a happily-ever-after. She understands that faith is a work in progress more exciting than any story she can dream up. You can find out more about her books at authorlisaphillips.com.

Books by Lisa Phillips

Love Inspired Suspense

Double Agent
Star Witness
Manhunt
Easy Prey
Sudden Recall
Dead End
Colorado Manhunt
"Wilderness Chase"
Desert Rescue
Wilderness Hunt

Secret Service Agents

Security Detail
Homefront Defenders
Yuletide Suspect
Witness in Hiding
Defense Breach
Murder Mix-Up

Visit the Author Profile page at LoveInspired.com for more titles.

WILDERNESS HUNT

LISA PHILLIPS

LOVE INSPIRED SUSPENSE
INSPIRATIONAL ROMANCE

LOVE INSPIRED® SUSPENSE
INSPIRATIONAL ROMANCE

ISBN-13: 978-1-335-58816-6

Recycling programs for this product may not exist in your area.

Wilderness Hunt

Love Inspired
22 Adelaide St. West, 41st Floor
Toronto, Ontario M5H 4E3, Canada
www.LoveInspired.com

Printed in U.S.A.

I called upon thy name, O Lord, out of the low dungeon.
—*Lamentations* 3:55

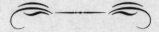

Huge thanks go to my author friends,
who make every book better with their input.
And to great dogs we will see again.

ONE

Smoke from a plane crash no one had been able to locate—yet—hung in the air. K-9 officer Kelly Wayne let out a short whistle. Her dog and partner, Nico, stopped and sank with her belly to the mountain path.

Kelly took up the slack in the long line and crouched beside her. The German shepherd was bred for police work, with the papers to prove it. Too bad she was stuck with a partner who had a spotty disciplinary record and the inability to cook.

The dog sniffed Kelly's hand, unaware what Kelly had sensed. If Nico could do something to earn playtime, she would. In whatever form that came. Nico meant victory, and in Kelly's experience the name held true. The dog wanted to win at everything.

She'd never had a better, or more reliable, partner.

Kelly had that same drive to prove to every-

one she and Nico could be an effective search
and rescue team out here. She'd been a cop for
six years, but a K-9 officer for just over a year
now. *Don't think about the past.* Finding that
plane crash would go a long way to Kelly and
Nico solidifying their place with the department.

When Nico laid her head on her front paws,
Kelly scratched her head. Then she made a click
sound with her throat. Nico was on four paws
a second later, alert and ready to work. *Sorry,
dog. No time to rest.* Not that the dog would
ever complain. She could outpace, outwork and
outlast Kelly any day of the week, and that was
no exaggeration.

But her human inadequacies were hardly the
point here.

They were miles from any road with a few
hours left until dark. Temps held steady, just
above forty. Her backpack contained plenty of
supplies, and they'd spent the night out in the
wilderness before, during training.

Kelly needed to know what caused her instincts to flare a moment ago. Nico had alerted
to something. Focusing on work didn't involve
thinking about her career before the K-9 unit
and Nico. Or the undercover work she'd been
so good at until she'd taken too many risks and

been kicked off the case. Then a fellow cop had died.

Tears burned her eyes. *What a mess.*

Kelly sniffed them back. "Smoke from the crash."

She needed to find that plane. All the cops in the local area knew now that the US Marshals had chartered the plane to take a protected witness to the local federal courthouse. There was a team inbound to deal with the crash, but it was the defendant of the case she was interested in.

Michael O'Callaghan needed to be taken down for ruining so many lives selling poison. The fact that the case connected to her being undercover and the loss of her partner during that operation had no bearing now. She'd said that to everyone she worked with so many times she could recite it.

Believing what she said was something different entirely.

Nico's head turned, and her nostrils flared. The dog's body tightened, and she stared to the left. Alert. Focused.

Kelly shortened the distance between them, coiling the long line in a big loop. They took the next few steps together. Kelly headed toward a downed tree in a group of berry bushes. She took cover, Nico right beside her, and waited to find out why the dog had alerted like that.

Seconds later two men crashed through the underbrush, talking.

"...nowhere near here."

"You're the one who said it was this way."

"I thought I saw something. That's what I said."

Both had jeans and jackets on. No gloves. One wore a ball cap. She'd met enough people since she moved here to know they weren't locals. One of the guys had tattoos on the backs of his fingers—and a gun in his hand. The other had scratches on his face like he'd rushed headlong into the brush.

Tattoo guy rubbed his jaw with his free hand. "Whatever you saw, it's not here."

"Then where'd it go?" the guy with the scratched face asked.

"Probably a deer or something."

Scratches said, "We could shoot it."

Kelly clenched her teeth. Two against one? Not good, even with Nico. The dog could take down both these guys, but the last thing she wanted to do was waste time when a federal witness was out here in need of help. Lost. Hurt probably, a result of the plane crash. She wouldn't get justice for Brett's death if the witness didn't show up to testify.

Her phone buzzed in her pocket. It was past time to check in with her chief.

Kelly kept watch on the two men.

"Come on. Let's keep moving," Tattoo guy said. "If we don't find that plane, we can't kill the witness."

"After we torture him for where he stashed the money," Scratch said. "That's my favorite part."

Tattoo guy huffed. "Then see something good next time. Or we don't get to have fun *or* get paid."

Kelly shuddered. Nico let out a high whine, sympathetic to what Kelly was going through. But she didn't need her partner to pity her for her inadequacies. They just needed to get the job done and find that plane before these guys did.

Tattoo guy spun around. "What was that?"

Kelly stilled.

"Bunch of nothin'."

Nico yawned.

They were close enough they'd see her if she didn't act first.

Kelly reached over and unclipped Nico's lead. She gave the hand signal to stay, then shoved up, her weapon drawn. "Police. Hands up."

Tattoo guy's lips curled up.

"Weapons down." Kelly shifted her feet to a steady stance. "Hands. Up."

"You're gonna arrest us?"

"Conspiracy is a crime."

"Your word against mine."

"Irrelevant," she said. "You're done out here."

He strode toward her. There was no chance she'd have Nico take him down. She'd leave her partner to deal with Scratches, who looked like he had no intention of dropping his gun.

Still, Tattoo guy was the lethal one out here.

"Stop!" Kelly squared her aim on his chest. "Drop that weapon and any others you're carrying."

He didn't lower the gun. He also didn't have it pointed at her.

But it would be up and aimed at the vest under her jacket in a split second.

Kelly gave the command for Nico to release from her stay and take down the assailant farther from her rather than closer. It had taken extensive training but came in handy even in search and rescue situations.

The dog burst from the brush and launched at Scratches, whose weapon flew through the air as seventy pounds slammed into him at high speed.

Tattoo guy pulled his trigger.

Kelly did the same.

She felt the bullet slam into her torso. Her body jerked and she fell backward, with no idea if her shot hit the target.

A new guy burst through the trees with a roar, swinging a tree branch above his head. He swayed as he came at Tattoo guy, blood trailing down his face. Glassy eyes. He slammed the branch into Tattoo guy's head and wood splintered.

Tattoo guy rallied fast. He tackled the guy, and they both went down. The guy who'd run up to them hit the ground and went still. Scratches grabbed his gun, spun around and leveled it at Nico.

"Don't!" Kelly scrambled around for her weapon. Where was it? Her chest felt like she'd been punched hard in the sternum.

"Let's go!" Tattoo guy hauled the unconscious man onto his shoulder. "We got him. Let's go." In his other hand he held the pistol he'd shot her with.

Kelly raised her hands. "Don't shoot my dog."

Scratches didn't pay her any attention.

"I said, 'Let's go,'" Tattoo guy ordered.

Scratches shifted. For a heartbeat Kelly was sure she was about to watch her partner die. Instead, Scratches turned and kicked Nico. The dog yelped and tumbled down the hill as the two men left with their prize—and the backpack she'd dropped.

Kelly ignored them and scrambled to see where Nico had landed. Her chest burned, but she wouldn't stop until she knew her partner was all right.

She glanced over her shoulder. They might have taken off, but they had to know she'd pursue them to the ends of the earth for hurting Nico.

The dog shook off the blow, but Kelly still checked where she'd been kicked and found the area tender. "You good?"

Nico barked.

"Ready?"

The dog turned around. Kelly clipped the leash on and found a glove on the ground that had to have fallen out of someone's pocket. Thanking God there was still a signal out here, she sent a text to her chief explaining everything while Nico moved tight to her side.

Kelly gave her the command to catch a scent from the glove, then said, "Nico, find."

Pain. It split his skull—or felt like it. He was... Nope, too much thinking. He gritted his teeth and breathed through the swell of pain.

Bile rose in his throat.

"He's awake."

His body shifted, bent over a man's shoulder. A second later he hit the ground. A low groan puffed out his lips.

"Well, Harrigan." The man's face swam into

view. This was not a guy he'd want to meet in a dark alley. Or in the middle of trees while a cold breeze pushed through the branches.

Harrigan. That sounded right. "What…" He didn't know what to say, and the need to swallow back sickness beckoned. He sucked in a few breaths and tried to figure out what was happening.

A flash of white teeth.

Green, like a military uniform.

But on a wild animal? That made no sense.

"She's got a bunch of stuff in here."

He found the man who spoke to his right. Light from between the clouds had him wincing against the pain. *Head hurts.*

The man had blood on his cheek and knuckles. Face flush, dark hair sticking up. He rummaged through a backpack, pulling out bottles of water and protein bars.

His stomach rumbled. The sky above him darkened, and he could hear running water.

A man stood over him.

He stared at the guy. "Who are you?" His brain definitely wasn't working, even if he had never met these guys before. He didn't know what had happened, or how he'd gotten all the way out in what looked like the middle of nowhere.

"Where am I? Why am I here?"

The guy over him shifted, set his boot on his chest and leaned down.

He wanted to breathe, but the man's weight constricted his chest. "Hey. Don't."

"Should've thought of that before you sold us out, Harrigan. Now you're testifying?"

Then the guy spat on him.

"Found a phone."

The guy pulled his weight off his chest and headed for the friend, who sat on a boulder beside a rushing river. "That a sat phone?"

"Looks like it." Backpack guy, with the scratches on his face, bit into a bar and tossed a phone into the river. "Want one of these?"

"Later." The guy lifted his chin.

"You think we have to worry about the lady cop?"

"We'd be idiots if we don't." He had tattoos on his hand and a gun in the back of his belt when he shifted. "We keep moving. Meet up with the others."

These two would kill him. But he didn't think it would happen straightaway. When it did, though, he wasn't going to be rescued. His body would be found later.

He wouldn't get to...

He needed to find...

Testify.

Pain rolled through his head. It was all he

could do to lift his arm and wipe his sleeve across his face.

He needed to get away, figure out help and a car. Something. Police, maybe the one they were talking about—a female cop.

Had he seen a woman?

Harrigan didn't know…if that was even his name. It felt right. It sounded right. *What is wrong with me?* His brain wouldn't make the connections. When he tried, it just made his head hurt more.

"What did you do to me?" He croaked the words out. He wanted to sit up, so he didn't look so helpless to these guys. He rolled and spotted a river. Trees flanked both sides.

He started to push off the ground.

Tattoo guy rushed over and kicked his shoulder.

He blinked up at the sky. His mind flashed again with the image of that dark animal and its white teeth. It lunged at him. Then a military uniform—but it was on the dog? That didn't make sense.

None of this did.

"Stay down," Tattoo guy said.

He breathed. While they weren't looking, he would try and rally his strength. Get up. Run from these guys, somehow.

Why did they want him? They knew who

he was, and they didn't like him. They would kill him.

All he had was that mental picture of the dog.

Not a wild animal. It had been *a dog*. He still had the scar on his forearm from a long time ago.

He lifted his hand and pulled his sleeve back. The scar was there. But even his name seemed...wrong somehow. There was only that skull-splitting pain when he tried to think past the dog's teeth and the green vest. An airplane flew overhead, high up in the sky like a passenger jet. They'd never be able to see him.

But a plane? That seemed connected somehow.

"You gonna call the boss?" one of the guys said.

Tattoo guy stilled. "Not yet."

"Are you serious? He'll kill us if we don't call right now and tell him everything." The guy shoved the backpack down and stood. He pulled a gun.

Tattoo guy shot him between the eyes.

The scratched guy landed in the dirt. Dead.

He had to get out of here. He scrambled to sit and gathered his legs under him. His shoes didn't look right. Something wet damped his shoulder. He reached up and touched his temple. The pain nearly sent him sprawling.

He fought back the sickness rising in his throat. He scrambled to stand and nearly swayed back onto the ground. He braced a hand on a rock.

He pushed off, taking the stone with him.

Tattoo guy held his gun. "I can't kill you yet. Not till you tell me everything."

Harrigan adjusted his grip on the rock. He pitched it at Tattoo guy and sprinted away. Toward the river. *No.* He wasn't thinking straight. He should've gone the other way.

Too late.

He splashed into the water and began wading across.

A gunshot spliced the air and sang past his ear. He yelped and started to run against the flowing water. He had to get across to the other side.

Tattoo guy tackled him.

His knees gave out and he face-planted into the water. The ice cold shocked his mind into clarity.

The guy rolled off. He went the other way and scrambled out of reach.

"Hey!" A woman called out from a distance.

Tattoo guy grabbed him, and he went under again. Thick fingers banded around his throat. He gasped for air but got only frozen water.

The man holding him jerked. The fingers slipped away, and the man was gone.

He tried to find the strength to get up.

He had none.

Someone grabbed his shirt and lifted his face above water. She was blonde and beautiful. Maybe the most beautiful woman he'd ever seen. Or was he in worse condition than he'd thought?

"You're really alive?" She shook her head. "Don't worry, Brett. I'll get you to that courtroom."

He frowned. *Brett.*

Was that his name?

TWO

"Brett?" The man blinked. "Is that my name?"

"I guess you hit your head or something." Kelly grabbed his arm, crouched and got under it. "Help me out, yeah?" She got him up on his feet and they waded out of the river.

Nico barked, bounding back and forth on the shore.

"You are a good girl, aren't you?"

The man grunted.

"She found you, by the way." *She's a true-blue bona fide hero.*

His whole body shivered beside her. "Seems like maybe you both did."

She found herself shaking from the cold as he had. "Let's just focus."

She didn't need Brett Harrigan to placate her. *So you're not dead.* She didn't know whether to be happy he was alive and testifying, or angry over what he'd done.

Six months on an undercover investigation,

her first shot to show her captain she could do serious police work—really make a difference. Brett had completely shut her out.

No notice. No explanation.

Nothing.

She helped him ease down to sit on the closest boulder. Eight feet away, a dead man lay with a bullet hole in his head. "Friend of yours?"

"The guy with the tattoos shot him."

Nico raced over, the only one completely dry. Kelly touched both sides of the dog's face and rubbed the way Nico liked. "Yes, you did. You really did find Brett."

She let go and Nico sat.

Kelly grabbed the backpack from the shore. She pulled out the bright yellow tennis ball and threw it directly at the ground three feet away. It bounced up in the air. Nico launched up and caught it on the first try.

Brett chuckled. "She seems fun."

"She's a cop. And a German shepherd."

The idea of small talk ignited a hot ball of anger in her stomach. She pushed all thoughts of the past away. *Focus.*

Kelly pulled out a space blanket. "Take off your shirt."

His pants were soaking wet as well, but there was only so much she could handle, and he would end up all scratched up after they walked out of here.

He'd turned so his back was to her and arched up to pull the T-shirt over his head. On the back of his shoulder was a faded tattoo—a military unit. Marine Corps. She couldn't get close enough to read the words and numbers. "I didn't know you served."

She wasn't going to mention the thick scar on his flank, which was as faded as the tattoo. He'd been shot.

Brett twisted around and she handed him the blanket. "Did I?"

He had a matching scar on his side, in front. One entry. One exit. Not only had he served, but he'd also been wounded. She knew nothing about this guy.

Well, that wasn't entirely true, was it?

Nico bounded back over.

"Loose."

The ball fell from her mouth and bounced on the ground. Kelly returned it to the backpack.

"You're the witness the marshals are taking to the federal courthouse, right?" Smoke from the plane wreckage was visible to the north. She wanted to check it out, but the priority here was getting the witness to safety.

She continued, "They faked your death so not even the cops you worked with knew it wasn't real." They'd buried him, and now here he stood.

He just stared at her and shivered.

Her backpack contained a clean shirt, XXL size since most people could get it on or at least wrap it around them. She handed it over. "I keep this for emergencies."

"Thanks." He shifted the blanket long enough to pull on the shirt for Bobby's Grill and their famous fry sauce, then settled the foil back over his shoulders. He let out a long sigh. "I have no clue who those guys are, or why I'm out here." He winced. "You called me Brett…but I have no idea if that's even my name."

She wanted to get mad. After all, it would serve him right to suffer a bit after what he'd done to her. But how was that fair? The alternative was to feel sorry for him. He probably wouldn't like pity any more than anger. "Let's get you to a hospital and we can figure out what's going on, yeah?"

He might need a brain scan. Hopefully he would make it back to safety, but it was a long walk to her car. Kelly knew she should pray about this. Cover what they were about to do by asking God for His will to be done.

But something in her stopped the words from forming.

They would get there under their own steam

anyway, so why did she need God's help when the outcome of that would be unknown? She'd rather trust what she knew—her and Nico and their ability to get the job done.

Then everyone else would see how capable they were as well.

"Seeing a doctor is probably a good idea." He frowned. "Do we know each other?"

Kelly lifted her chin. "I thought we did. I guess I was wrong." She slid the straps over her shoulders and clicked her tongue for Nico. "Heel."

The dog was at her side, ready to move with her a second later.

"Are we just going to leave this guy here?"

Kelly pressed her lips together. "Let's see if he has ID or something on him. We can let my chief know he's out here when we get to safety—or a spot with a phone signal—and about the guy who floated away."

She took the dead man's picture with her phone and then went through his pockets. She'd rather have done it with gloves. Thankfully nothing poked her, and she found a photo in one pocket. A picture of Brett, the man the O'Callaghan family wanted dead before he could testify against their patriarch.

She could see the outline of a wallet in his

back pocket. Kelly dug it out and found a driver's license. "Carl Wallace."

Not exactly a resounding piece of evidence pointing to the O'Callaghan crime family. She stuck the wallet in her backpack. "Ready to—"

Brett patted his pockets, front and back.

"Everything okay?"

"Just looking to see if I have anything on me. Like ID or…anything." His hands remained empty.

"You really don't remember who you are?"

"I'm not lying."

It wasn't like she thought that—at least not about this.

All she wanted was to show everyone she could do this job. His cutting her out of that undercover investigation had almost destroyed her career. Had he even thought of that before he took all the evidence with him, and the marshals faked his death?

Kelly sighed. If she got him back to safety, she would be the hero for a second. This guy she had barely been friends with could go back to his life, and she'd know she was the one who saved him from two shooters.

Bonus: he would testify and the O'Callaghans would be destroyed.

Pretty much a win-win as far as she was concerned. Just so long as he quit giving her those lost-puppy eyes and her heart didn't squeeze at the thought of him being out here alone—in danger, with no idea who he was.

Kelly set off, before this whole thing got any worse. "Let's get moving. It'll be dark soon."

She had called him Brett, but he wasn't convinced that was his name. Even if it felt familiar in a lot of ways. Close and comforting.

Maybe it *was* his name.

The men who'd carried him to the river had called him Harrigan. Now he looked down at the one who lay dead. Clearly not the alpha of the pair, as he had been shot so suddenly by his associate, the one now floating down the river.

He wasn't going to trust that the man was dead and wouldn't come back. Some latent instinct said he shouldn't believe when there was still a possibility the guy was alive. And when the risk had life or death for him attached to it, there was no reason to be caught unawares.

She turned at the tree line. "Are you coming?"

Even the dog looked back at him.

Brett—he may as well think of himself like that, as it seemed so familiar—took long strides that ate up the distance between them. After that dip in the freezing river, he was ready to jog away the cold and the tension in his muscles. But his soaked jeans didn't make that a good idea.

"Okay?" She studied him, probably trying to figure out if he would collapse and she'd have to carry him again the way she'd gotten him out of the river.

He nodded. "I'm good to go."

"Okay, sailor."

He frowned, but there was no time to ask her what that meant. She moved fast, and he had to work to keep up with her and the animal. "What is your dog's name?"

"This is Nico." Before he could ask his next question, she said, "She's a police search and rescue dog. Which came in handy when your plane crashed in our backyard." She motioned to the trees around them.

A plane crash? He frowned. "Did you say something before about the marshals?"

"They are transporting a federal witness to court so he can testify against a dangerous crime family." There was a thread of tension in her tone. He wasn't quite sure what to make of it.

"Is that a bad thing?" He couldn't figure this woman out. But part of him wanted to.

"Not if we get you there."

His eyebrows rose as he followed her. They picked their way up a tiny path probably meant for deer. "You think I'm the witness?"

"Why else would you be out here, running from gunmen trying to kill you? Everyone thought you were dead. Where else would you be but WITSEC?"

"Those two guys said they were going to torture me. Maybe for information?" It was hard to remember what they'd been talking about. He still felt the same disorientation that had been there when he'd woken up with no memory of how he got here—let alone who he was.

She glanced back over her shoulder. "Do you know what they want?"

"I'm sure I'd tell you. If I remembered."

She closed her mouth and frowned. "They mentioned missing money."

He felt the same as her. Frustrated, confused by this whole situation and wondering why all this was happening. Then again, maybe she knew exactly why *she* felt like this and had a handle on the whole deal. She did seem efficient and focused, something he appreciated.

Regardless of the fact he was unsteady, achy and had been through the wringer the last few hours, she didn't baby him. He got the feeling he would've hated it if she had.

Instead, she'd assumed he was capable when he said he was and trusted him to watch her back as they made their way through the woods. He frowned. "Where are we going?"

She'd mentioned the hospital, but he didn't see one anywhere around them. There was nothing but trees and mountains. It didn't seem strange to be out in nature, even given the circumstances.

"My car is in this direction."

"How far is the walk?" He got the feeling there was a reason she hadn't given him a specific distance.

"I'm not exactly sure, and I don't have a cell signal to find out where we are on the maps app. So we're going on my best guess, which is that it's about four miles. Give or take."

"Fine by me." His head didn't feel great. All it was doing was making him nauseous. He remembered that guy throwing her satellite phone downriver.

"I still have water and protein bars left if you need anything."

"Thanks. I'll let you know." Something about her offer made him want to get where they were going without needing anything. He wondered if he was the kind of person who was so bullheaded they ignored their own health and safety to get the job done. All to prove to everyone that they could.

Maybe at one point in his life. He wasn't sure if it was necessary now.

There was a shift in his awareness. Something to his left. "Seven o'clock."

The woman turned to look.

"I just realized I don't know your name."

"Kelly Wayne." She frowned at him. "What's at seven o'clock?"

He felt it again, that same shift. "If you don't want to battle it out with two new guys, then we need to hide."

She pointed to the right. "Let's go over there. That tree and all the bushes."

He led the way, so she could protect his back this time—with the gun holstered on her hip if necessary. The dog sped up to trot beside him, and he got the feeling that had happened to him before. But running with empty hands didn't seem right. The way not carrying a pack on his back was also odd.

I didn't know you served.

He needed to figure out who he was, tattoo or not. Or find someone who knew him. Kelly seemed to, if his name really was Brett, but they had bigger priorities now than reassuring him that he wasn't going crazy. That he would remember.

Was he really a protected federal witness? He had no idea if that was right or not.

He rounded the downed tree and crouched out of sight. The dog panted, her tongue hanging long from her mouth. He scratched under her chin, and she leaned her head to the side so he could focus on one spot.

Kelly crouched on the other side of them.

Voices rang out. A shout he could hear, but not the words that were spoken.

He hissed and said a reflexive, *"Platz."*

The dog hit the deck, belly to the dirt. He ducked his head, frowning at his use of that word. He peered between branches but couldn't see much. There was something all too familiar about being pinned down. He didn't want to think about it too much. His head was pounded.

"We might need to make a break for it," Kelly whispered. "But it looks like they're going the other direction."

He nodded. "I can run whenever you're ready."

He didn't want to face down men determined to torture and murder him. Not just because he had no way to protect himself. Something about Kelly made him want to stick by her side.

She was the only person who had helped him so far.

He didn't want to leave her.

"Okay, they've headed away from us. Quick and quiet, yeah?"

She said that word a lot. *Yeah.* Like she didn't have the confidence to give a command. And from a woman determined to protect him? He'd have followed her lead at any time.

"Go." That was the command.

He lifted from his crouch, high enough he could run, and took off between the trees.

A gunshot exploded in the distance.

"Go!"

THREE

Everything in Kelly's world eclipsed down to a tunnel where only she and Brett, along with Nico, existed. That, and the knowledge they had to get away from the people behind them. She'd been so sure these new shooters were unaware the three of them hid. Clearly she'd jumped the gun and moved too fast. Or just plain blown it.

A bullet whizzed past her head and embedded itself in a tree. Shards of bark sprayed up, and one caught her cheek. She hissed at the sting but kept going. There would be time enough to deal with everything later.

She had to get Brett to safety.

He was the only thing that mattered. Otherwise the O'Callaghans would continue to get away with profiting from crime and destroying people's lives. Michael O'Callaghan was out on a bond worth millions—and he would stay free if Brett didn't show up for the trial.

Brett glanced over his shoulder, his gaze hard. She was right behind him, Nico up ahead. They were good. They could do this.

Another shot rang out. She heard someone shout but just focused on running.

Then she heard the words "Don't kill them" yelled over the distance between her and the men firing.

The voice was familiar, but she couldn't place it. Not when her future and everything she wanted hung in the balance between running and remaining here, where they would be killed. One of the O'Callaghans, maybe. There was no time to look back and check.

If these guys weren't going to keep shooting at her and Brett, there was no reason to take cover and fire back at them, something she wouldn't have minded. But taking on several people solo, when she had a federal witness to protect, wasn't what she should be doing.

Her gun remained in its holster, and she focused on getting Brett and Nico out of here. The two of them were far more valuable than her.

They reached a peak and crested the top. Brett just kept running. Nico did a four-legged scramble to get downhill. Kelly tried to slow but her boot clipped a rock. Pain shot through her foot.

She caught herself on one knee and planted

her hands on the ground, but her momentum meant she kept going. Gravel and pine needles scraped her palms.

She cried out and lifted her hands. Her body tumbled sideways, and she started to roll.

Before she got a full rotation in, someone grabbed her elbow. An arm snaked under her body, and she was hauled up. Brett lifted her to her feet, still going downhill. He slowed to pick his way along the rapidly descending ground.

At the bottom, she spotted a creek. Likely a tributary that fed into the main river she'd pulled him out of. Kelly shivered at the sight of it.

He held on to her until they were at the base of the hill. "I could go back up and see if they're still following us."

She shook her head. "Let's make our way along the creek and see what we can find."

She was completely turned around, as well as disoriented from falling. Her hands stung something fierce, making her bite her lip just to contend with the pain. It was better than crying. Raised by her dad, she hadn't ever been allowed to cry. These days she thought it might make her feel better. But part of her wondered if she started, would she ever stop?

It was much better to keep her focus, and that

cool head her dad told her to have. One foot in front of the other. Always moving.

"Okay," he said. "Stick together. That's a good idea."

She set off. He hovered beside her, his hands ready to catch her if she fell.

She wasn't entirely sure she was comfortable switching their roles. She was a police officer, and he was the protected federal witness. She was the one who was supposed to deliver him back to the US Marshals, who would take over the job of keeping him safe.

So far she hadn't seen a single marshal out here from the plane.

It made her wonder where they all were and how he had ended up in the wilderness alone. Hunted by men determined to capture and kill him. WITSEC wasn't a life she would have chosen for herself. Given his choice in cutting her out of that undercover assignment, she hadn't been given a choice.

No one would deny Brett wasn't doing the absolute right thing by testifying and taking down the O'Callaghans once and for all.

Nico ambled over to them from her spot, apparently considering the danger passed. Maybe she didn't hear or smell anything. That was a good sign. Dog senses were so much more efficient than a human's, and she was willing to trust Nico's instincts.

Her K-9 sniffed her hands.

She didn't pet her dog, as her throbbing palms were damp. And she didn't think it was sweat. "I know. It hurts."

She scanned the area. They were a little higher now than they had been, and she heard nothing from the gunmen in hot pursuit.

She wasn't going to assume they were safe even though they were in the middle of the woods. Kelly shook her head and tried to figure a way to make her mind make sense. They needed to be out of danger.

He said, "Let's find somewhere to sit."

She glanced over at Brett. "We just decided we would head up that way." She motioned with her hand. Bad idea. That stinging pain shot up her wrist now.

"Your hand." Brett gasped and grabbed it. "Tell me you have a first aid kit in your backpack."

He opened her palm gently, tugging on her fingers, and hissed.

"It doesn't hurt that bad."

"Good. Then it won't *hurt that bad* when we wipe them and put some ointment on."

She wanted to pout. "You're mean."

A low rumble shook his chest under the T-shirt.

At least he'd taken it the way she intended. "What are we going to do about those guys? They're probably racing after us right now."

"Let's walk a little more and find somewhere to hole up and do this. We need a spot where they'll walk right by us."

"A place like that sounds great." Even after it got dark, they would be able to stay guarded until either they were found or it was morning and they could get away.

"In the meantime, I don't think you can fire your weapon with that hand." He lifted her other and saw it was the same. "Will you give me your gun?"

Kelly felt her brows rise. "You think I'm gonna hand you my duty weapon?"

"I think you need to let me help you protect us."

"Because I can't?"

Brett said, "There's no way you can pull the trigger with your hands like that. It'll be excruciating."

It was on the tip of her tongue to make him promise he wouldn't shoot her. But that was ridiculous. He'd been a cop even if he was now in witness protection. He didn't have any reason to hurt her.

"Fine. If something happens, you can pull it out."

He slid her weapon from its holster. "Something already happened, Kelly. Whether either of us likes it or not."

He knew she didn't like it. She also didn't say anything. But what was there to say? It was plain enough that he was right, and even if the dog seemed to have relaxed, he had no intention of doing the same.

Whether he was this Brett person she'd known or not, he was going to keep his eyes peeled.

Not that he thought she was lying about knowing him. She didn't seem like that kind of woman. But he also wasn't going to be fooled by the police shield on her belt.

Even if she was the only person who'd been nice to him, he still didn't know her. He didn't know anybody right now. Everything in him insisted on heightened awareness.

It would be exhausting living every day like this. But with everything that'd happened, it was the most prudent course of action right now. The one that might save their lives.

God, go with us.

It was natural to call on the best help he knew. The One he trusted no matter what.

She said, "Which way?"

He couldn't hear anyone coming and didn't see their pursuers, but had they really lost those men so quickly? He wasn't sure. "Let's head across the creek and go up the other side. I'd rather have the high ground."

She set off first. "Nico, heel."

He followed her, wondering about that word he'd used before. *Platz*. The word that caused the dog to lie down in response. He didn't know how he knew it. Or really what the word meant.

As frustrating as it was being so confused, he couldn't let his thoughts rabbit trail. They had to keep moving and get to a position they could defend.

He scanned as they went, looking behind him every few feet just to make sure no one was on their six.

He saw a couple of options but wanted to get farther away. He'd have to put the gun down in order to doctor her hands. That meant they had to be somewhere relatively safe.

About a mile or so up, the trail snaked back across the creek, a place where animals could take a drink. The rocks were slick. Nico trotted across easily until Kelly told her to drink, and then the animal lapped at the water. Content.

"I've always liked dogs. Even if one bit me once."

Kelly started to turn. Her foot shifted on a rock, and she tipped over. He lurched forward and caught her in his arms. One of his shoes splashed into the water, but he was already so soaked he barely noticed except for the renewed feeling of cold.

She blinked and looked up at him from within the hold of his arms.

"Hey." He didn't know what to say. "You okay?"

"Yes, thank you." Kelly got her feet under her. "Can you let go of me?"

She stepped out of his arms to cast a long shadow on the creek. He looked over at where the sun was setting behind the mountains. "It won't be long until dark."

"This whole place is crawling with O'Callaghan's men, and we have no idea how many are out here." She shot him a look. "So let's keep moving, shall we?"

Did that mean she wasn't going to express any gratitude, because he'd just saved her from getting dunked? The last thing he wanted was to watch her float away down the river. This part wasn't exactly deep. It was maybe six inches in this spot and probably a foot of depth on either side of what amounted to a low bridge of stones they'd used to cross.

A familiar frustration rose in him. It had

nothing to do with the fact he couldn't remember who he was. Something about this woman, or maybe all women everywhere, brought out the worst in him.

He had no idea what it meant.

Maybe Kelly knew, since she'd met him before. Could she tell him why it seemed that every time she decided to do things her way it frustrated him more than it should?

The woman was only doing her job.

It was probably better if he left it alone. At least until they got somewhere safe. Right now he needed to focus.

"How about over there?" Kelly waved a hand up the hill. "Looks like some kind of cave."

If there was enough ventilation, they would be able to build a fire. Getting warm sounded like a fantastic idea right now. Though it wasn't like he could have dry clothes. Other than what she'd given him.

"Did I thank you for the T-shirt?"

She shook her head. "You were a little distracted at the time. But you're welcome." The dog wandered around the cave but made no noise. "There's no one in there. She would have alerted if there was."

"Good enough for me."

Kelly flipped on a flashlight. "Can you hold this?"

They moved deeper into the cave, and he saw it was essentially a small room chipped out of the rock. Or naturally occurring. A place to shelter from the outside world.

Thankfully nothing was currently sheltering here—like a bear.

"Do you have bandages and antiseptic cream?" He shone the light around while she sat and carefully lifted items out.

"I have both. But no hands with which to use them."

He sat in a position that meant he could see the entrance. Nico lay down and put her head on her paws. He laid the gun where he could grab it at a moment's notice if needed. Then he tore open several packets and got to work on her palms.

He held her hand in his and dabbed at the mess of one palm with a wipe. "Is this okay?"

"Yep." The word was short.

He looked at her and saw tears had gathered in the corners of her eyes. "It's fine if you cry. No one is going to judge you."

"I'm not going to cry. I'm a cop."

He wondered what that was supposed to mean. "So what's the plan, Officer Wayne?" He figured if she could focus on what they would do next, it would take her mind off the stinging pain in her hands.

"I want to make a run for it, but maybe that's just the anxiety talking."

"It might be good to stay long enough to rest and then head out." Soon it would be dark, and then it would be best to leave first thing in the morning. "Did you pack breakfast?"

"I'd love my satellite phone, but it's not here."

"They tossed it in the river."

She'd been here looking for him when those two gunmen had set upon her.

He'd intervened. He was sure of that much, but also just as certain he couldn't remember anything before that.

Kelly blinked up at him with tearful eyes.

Before she could say anything, Nico jumped up to stand.

Kelly whispered, "Someone is outside."

FOUR

Nico began to growl. Kelly held up her hand and shifted to stand. She winced. The cuts on her hand stung even with the numbing ointment Brett had smeared on them. Still, she didn't want Nico to race out there determined to do her job if someone was outside. Her dog needed backup.

Kelly lowered her hand. Nico sat, everything about her still alert. The dog wasn't going to relax, even if Kelly told her to. She was in full protection mode—something Kelly loved about her.

Brett moved to stand with his back to the wall at the entrance and looked out.

Would the men outside notice the cave and consider it worth checking out?

He held her gun at the ready. It was different from how she'd seen him do that before. Then again, nearly everything about him right now seemed…off. For whatever reason, he wasn't much like the man she had known from that undercover operation. Except in appearance.

Kelly crept to the opposite side of the entrance. Out of sight. Ready to do…something. Maybe kick someone. Anything else would require her hands and be extremely painful given both palms were a mess of abrasions.

"Do you see them?" The voice was male, calling to his associates.

"There's not much over here." The second man was farther away.

Would they walk right past the cave entrance and see nothing? *Lord, hide us.* After all that running, it would be amazing to feel safe finally. God could do that for them.

"I'm calling in!" the first guy called. A few quiet seconds went by, and all Kelly heard was the rush of air in her ears. "Yeah, it's me." He paused. "Some blonde. A cop with a dog."

Kelly's heart sank.

"Yeah, send it."

She frowned at Brett. Did he have a better idea than her about what was happening outside?

The man said, "Yeah, I think that's her. I only saw her from a distance, but it looks like the same woman. Is that the one?" His voice moved, as though he walked by the cave entrance. "If I see her again, she's dead. Got it."

The world started to tilt around her.

Kelly put out a hand and touched its back to the cold wall of the cave beside her. The jagged stone and dirt poked the bandage Brett had put on her injuries.

She forced herself to stay where she was. Took in a long breath, held it, then pushed the air out slowly. She didn't know how long it was before Brett came over.

"I think they're gone." He frowned. "Do you know what that was about? It seemed like they know who you are."

Energy drained from her. He was the one who'd been hurt and didn't remember his own name. The one who'd been dunked in the river. She'd saved him—after he saved her. Now she didn't know who was saving who, but it sure seemed like Brett was the one taking the lead here.

She had to get a handle on herself. One tumble and she was freaking out? That wasn't going to get them to safety. She had to snap out of this funk quickly and do her job. Be the cop protecting the federal witness, not allowing the federal witness to protect her.

Kelly went to the cave entrance and listened for a moment before she peered in both directions.

She moved back to where Brett waited. "I

think they're gone, but we should stay here. It's getting dark. Moving around at night might be a good way to go unseen, but it's also dangerous."

He nodded. "Agreed."

Kelly said, "We can sleep in shifts, keep watch and leave at daybreak." There was no room for discussion or argument in her tone, and she was fine with that. She crouched by her backpack and pulled out water.

He had to twist off the cap for her before doing the same with his own. It diminished the effect of her taking command of the situation, but she couldn't let that bother her.

Brett eased himself to sit with his back to the wall. "My head is pounding."

She found a bottle of over-the-counter pain meds and tossed it to him. "Might not even dent it, but it's better than nothing until we can get you to a hospital."

"Thanks." He swallowed a couple. "I think I need to know what's going on here."

She frowned. "What do you mean?"

He lifted a hand, then let it fall to his lap. At that moment he looked as exhausted as she felt. "I have no idea who *I* even am."

"Nothing has come back to you?"

Nico wandered over and lay down beside Kelly, her back to the outside of Kelly's leg.

She scratched the dog's side as best she could with a bandaged hand.

"Can you tell me who these people are?" *And what they want with me.* His question went unspoken.

However, now she supposed it was that the O'Callaghans wanted both of them, not just him.

He said, "Pretend I know nothing and tell me about them."

She supposed that was a fair request. "Wouldn't that be a form of witness tampering? I could skew your testimony if I feed you information."

"Whether it is or not, I need input, and everything is just blank." He let out a long sigh.

She nodded but pulled out her phone first. "My battery is getting low. I need to see if I can get a signal."

She moved to the entrance and waved the phone close to the outside. "I have a bar. It's worth a—"

Brett slapped the phone out of her hand.

He stared at her. Then the phone.

She frowned. "What was—"

"No calls." Everything in him screamed that her calling anyone was a horrible idea.

Kelly took a step back, shutters falling over her expression. "What was that, Brett?"

"How do you even know that's my name?" He struggled to keep from yelling. They didn't want to draw attention to their whereabouts, but he was about to lose it.

What was wrong with him? Aside from the obvious fact he could remember nothing. Like that wasn't enough?

He wanted to kick the cave wall. Get rid of this frustration. The second she'd dug out that phone and mentioned calling the cops he'd completely freaked. Like, red lenses over his eyes and a total eclipse of panic. He had no idea why he'd reacted like that.

Kelly folded her arms. "I know your name because I know you."

"Okay, but I don't know *you*."

"Yes, you do." She sighed. "Maybe it's latent, and you have reason to be paranoid. But deep down I'd think you know you can trust me."

He pushed out a breath and turned to pace the cave. "What am I even doing here?"

Maybe it had been building since the river when he'd tried to remember who he was. When that tattooed man shot his associate right in front of him, or when Kelly herself had insinuated she could tell him whatever she wanted to sway what he believed and affect a whole federal case.

Him, a material witness?

None of it was right. "This whole situation is bizarre."

"I'm sorry. It is part of the deal you signed as an undercover officer and when you agreed to testify."

"Except I can't remember any of that." He looked from her to the cave entrance. "So how can I possibly testify?"

Night had fallen, and dusk crept into the cave. Soon enough it would be pitch-black. Any light they made would be visible to the outside—if anyone remained to look for it.

Maybe all the shooters had gone to a hotel for the night. They certainly hadn't had camping equipment. It seemed like Kelly was the one most prepared to be out here, even with her dying phone battery.

He swiped it up. The screen of her cell was cracked across the middle. "I'm sorry I hit it out of your hand."

"Thank you. I appreciate you saying that."

"Can we sit?" He motioned to the cave as though chairs awaited them. "Will you tell me what you know about me and everything that's going on?"

He felt like he was blind in a way. However, blind people probably dealt with it with a lot more grace than he was. Memory blind. Was that a thing?

Something else he didn't know.

She studied him long enough that he wondered if she would turn him down. He might've just ruined everything between them with that one reaction.

"Okay." She sighed. "I need to sit anyway."

He did as well but wasn't as eager to admit it.

Nico hadn't roused more than to lift her head. Considering she could spring into action any second, maybe the dog wasn't entirely relaxed. He wondered if the lack of aggression meant she didn't consider him a threat.

That was good, right?

He figured Kelly needed a place to start her story. "You said I'm a federal witness. Who am I supposed to testify against?"

Kelly flinched. "If you can't remember before you're supposed to testify, there will be a big problem."

"I'll tell everyone it isn't your fault." He was the one who'd jumped that guy to save her and Nico even though he didn't know them and had no weapon except a tree branch. It wasn't like she was at fault for him being out here.

She shrugged. "It was Nico that found you, so I doubt I'll have much to complain about. Unless they decide to give her to someone else." Kelly's face crumpled. Before he could say anything, she waved a bandaged hand. "I don't want to get into all of that. I don't know why I said it."

"We all react differently to stress." The cave blurred in front of him. "I've seen grown men cry in their first firefight. When the air fills with smoke so you're basically blind, and bullets are flying around. One near miss can send you into panic mode." He blinked and the cave walls came back into focus. "How do I know that?"

"I'm guessing the answer has something to do with the Marine Corps tattoo on the back of your shoulder." Her face softened.

He didn't want pity. He wanted to look at the tattoo, only that would be next to impossible. Kelly might be his only ally out here, but she wasn't inviting him to more than her profession- alism.

He couldn't even defend himself.

Kelly said, "You never told me about being a marine, by the way. So maybe we didn't know each other as well as I thought." It didn't seem like that bothered her too much, but he wasn't sure he read her right.

She continued, "We both worked for the same precinct in west Chicago. The O'Callaghans ran entire neighborhoods. The two of us went in undercover and tried to get them to accept us as part of their operation. Work our way up."

Undercover cops. Chicago police department. Was that his life?

He managed to say, "What happened?"

"You cut me out. Six weeks of work, and suddenly I'm being reassigned like I was never there." She looked at Nico. "You are discovered dead, and every time I ask questions about what happened I get the runaround. I'm transferred to Records and tied to a desk. I swallowed that for two weeks before I applied for a position out here."

"Why Montana?"

"My dad lives here." She swallowed.

He thought for a second there was more to it. Maybe involving her mom, but she continued before he could ask.

"I figured being closer was a good idea, but this department..." She shook her head. "That isn't important right now. All I know is I got shut out, and then suddenly the O'Callaghans are all getting arrested." She shot him an earnest look like he'd have any idea what she was talking about. "They've got the son out on bail awaiting trial, and I'm sure the whole family is about to go down as a result."

"So I'm not testifying against all of them? Just one guy."

She shrugged. "I've been too busy training with Nico and getting the chief here to make us a permanent part of the department to do any more digging. Every time I did before, I was stonewalled."

She'd said something about a plane crash earlier. Could it really be a coincidence that it had gone down right in her proverbial backyard?

He said, "Seems like a huge fluke that I'd run into you of all people." There was another option, though. "Or the crash could've been intentional, and I was *supposed* to run into you."

"Why would that be?" Kelly frowned, but it was getting harder to see her face in the dark.

"I have no idea." And not just because he couldn't remember.

The truth was none of her story made sense.

His eyes grew heavy. Then came that falling sensation. He tried to fight the pull of sleep but couldn't.

An engine hummed under him.

Alarms blared. He opened his eyes and saw a man stride down the aisle. "Strap in. This thing is going down."

"What? We're crashing?" He lifted his gaze to watch the man and saw his face right before turning away.

"Just buckle up," the guy said. But that wasn't what had his attention.

The man's face was exactly the same as his.

FIVE

"Ready?" Kelly swung the backpack onto her shoulders and just about managed to hide how much her hands stung this morning.

He nodded but said nothing.

Kelly sighed. He'd been like this since he woke up a few minutes ago, starting out of what she imagined had been a nightmare. Unwilling to talk about it while she fed Nico.

She studied him as he folded up the space blanket. "It's going to be cold outside."

He shook his head. "Silver is too visible."

Despite the objection on the tip of her tongue, she turned so he could stuff it in her backpack. Supplies were dwindling. They needed to get to safety without much more going wrong.

Enough had happened already, and it had kept her up half the night even when she was supposed to be asleep. Mostly thinking about that money those guys were after. And the fact they planned to kill her.

Brett had made a good partner so far since the plane went down. She still felt like something was off about him. It was probably just the fact he needed her help.

The vulnerability of not having his memories meant he was forced to trust her word. Not to mention she was so much more…aware of him.

That certainly hadn't been the case before.

"Are you sure you're okay?" Kelly asked.

He didn't meet her gaze. "Just a nightmare." He shook his head. "I want to tell you, but made no sense so what's the point? It was like looking in a mirror—during a plane crash." He strode outside.

Kelly rushed to catch up, wondering at his words.

The sun had barely risen, and it wasn't even six in the morning. She clipped on Nico's long lead. The dog would have some slack to sniff anything she wanted. Nico had worked enough the last twenty-four hours, and every dog trainer knew it wasn't always about work. Sometimes a dog just needed to be a dog.

Except the situation was far from over.

"Which way?"

She glanced over at him and saw his face in profile, the dark expression he'd been wearing since he woke up. "How is your head?"

He shrugged one shoulder. "We should just get moving."

It was on the tip of her tongue to apologize, probably sarcastically, for bothering to be concerned about his well-being. But he was right, so she closed her mouth and looked around. "Before I saw those two guys yesterday, I was using the maps on my phone to keep my bearing of which direction I had gone. But I don't recognize this."

And her satellite phone had been tossed down the river.

He glanced around and looked at the sky. "We could figure out which way is north."

"The town is west of the wooded area where the plane crashed. It's hundreds of miles of mountain terrain, so it's no guarantee. But if we go that way we will at least be heading in the right direction." She set off, using the rising sun as a guide. "I was also sharing my location with my boss yesterday. Maybe he sent some of my coworkers out to look for me when I never checked in last night."

"You think so?"

Kelly sighed. "Everyone's looking for you and the US marshals. They probably figure they'll come across me at some point in the search if I did get lost."

"So we can look out for cops as well? What about volunteer search and rescue?"

She hissed out a breath. "I hope there aren't civilians out here with all the gunmen we've seen."

"Do you think the ones we heard outside last night are the same ones who were chasing us yesterday after Tattoo guy shot his associate?" Before she could answer he continued, "I don't know why you would know the answer to that when I don't. Sorry."

Kelly glanced over her shoulder where he walked behind her. "Did you just apologize to me? Maybe that's twice, now that I think about it."

He shrugged. "Why would that be so surprising?"

She scrunched up her nose the way her dad always told her looked ridiculous. Brett's gaze zeroed in on it, and his lips curled up.

Kelly whirled back around and kept going.

"Answer me this. When we knew each other before…" He went silent.

He was quiet long enough that she wanted to glance at him again, but that would be a bad idea. This was a Brett she'd never met before.

"Did we ever…?"

"I wasn't attracted to you," Kelly said. Did he think she had been? "And right now I'm a cop, out here doing my job. You and I are professionals. And besides, everything doesn't always have to be about relationships." Her cheeks heated, and she realized what she'd said.

He kept quiet, which was probably a good decision. She had no idea what she'd say next and was probably better off keeping her mouth shut. Maybe they could walk in silence. Even if it was a hundred miles there was nothing they needed to say.

Nico shifted.

Kelly pulled up some of the slack on the lead, just in case the dog had caught a scent.

A second later, Nico came to a stop. She lifted her nose and sniffed.

Then sat.

"What does that mean?"

Kelly said, "How do you know that means anything?"

He frowned.

"Sorry." She rolled her shoulders. "Yes, it means something. Nico had some training before I got her. We've mainly worked on scent tracking so far, though there are several variations of it. That, and a couple of protection tactics just in case she needs to defend the two of us." Kelly walked up beside the K-9. "Nico, seek."

The dog bolted off the side of the trail into the

grass and trees. Pine needles littered the ground. She would need to recheck Nico's paws today in case she had something embedded there that would cause pain or injury.

She used the seek command whenever Nico had discovered something on her own and alerted. The word *find* she saved for when the job required Nico to catch a scent from an item— usually clothing—and locate that specific person.

Nico had saved an older man lost in a state park just last week.

"See anything?" She needed him to be as aware as her, considering the fact armed bad guys roamed these woods.

"Up ahead. On the ground."

Nico had caught a scent. Kelly said, "Good girl. Seek."

The dog led her to where a man lay on the ground. Blood soaked the dirt under his head. A badge for the US Marshals on his belt, that big shiny silver star.

Nico sat.

"Do you think the guy who took a trip down the river shot him?"

Kelly crouched and dug in her backpack for the yellow tennis ball. "It's possible. But unless we have a ballistics report, we can't say with any surety."

He figured that was true, at least without witnessing it themselves. "Want me to check his pockets?"

"Yes, please."

He kept the gun out. There was no way he would tuck it in his belt, even if that put it within reach when it was the only weapon either of them had. Though, he supposed in a way the dog was a weapon.

He rounded the body and crouched on the far side.

"Recognize him?"

He shook his head.

That dream had left him reeling, trying to figure out why he'd been staring at himself in the mirror on a plane about to go down, having some kind of bizarre experience. He didn't know what to think about it. Only being here with Kelly grounded him.

Had he always felt that way about her?

Maybe one day he would remember. That could leave him disappointed as easily as it might mean there was something between them on his end. Maybe she'd broken his heart and that was why he had her kicked off the case.

He didn't know he was a cop—or had been at some point. Neither did he feel like he should be a witness. Or anything else, like a former marine.

The word *former* didn't sound right. As if he would ever *not* be a marine. But how could he be a cop as well? Nothing he was thinking made any sense.

He checked the guy's jacket pockets. The dead man's shoes were not meant to traverse the woods. At least he had running shoes. Though boots like Kelly's would be better.

He found a cell phone and figured the man's wallet would be in his pants pocket on the front or underneath his body.

She said, "Does that phone have juice?"

Considering his reaction to the last cell phone, he was braced this time. When the rush of fear came, he simply checked the screen and handed it over. "Battery and signal."

He shivered, and not from the cold. Maybe these were the latent effects of having been in a plane crash. But how would he know if that was true?

"Can you get into the phone?" He glanced at her and Nico trotted over, the yellow ball in her mouth. "Loose."

The dog dropped the ball onto the dirt.

He tossed it a couple of feet away and the dog bounded after it.

"It's password protected, maybe with his thumbprint?" But Kelly didn't hand it back. "I can still make an emergency call."

He didn't want to go through a dead man's pockets any longer, so he straightened and surveyed around them. He spotted a couple of deer in the trees—a doe and her baby enjoying the early hours. No gunmen anywhere that he could see.

"Yes, this is Officer Kelly Wayne and I need to report that I found a dead deputy US marshal." She paused. "He was shot in the head before I got here. No, I have no idea where *here* actually is and there's no way anyone can bring in a helicopter... Yes, I'm aware the county doesn't have a helicopter... No, I'd rather not sit here with the dead body when there are armed men and people who need protection in these woods. I still have a job to do."

Wasn't she going to mention the fact he was with her?

It could be because he hadn't reacted well to her calling in yesterday. Was she seriously considering his feelings and situation after he had cut her out of an undercover investigation?

He didn't know whether to be impressed or nervous over her ability to strategize. He definitely didn't want to be on the receiving end of it if he was her target. And after everything that'd happened, he couldn't help wondering if all this was something other than a simple plane crash.

"Thank you." She lowered the cell from her

ear. "I'm going to leave the phone, and they're going to use it to lead them here to get him. The Marshals have a lot more resources than our tiny police department, and they're already on their way."

That meant more good guys in these woods. Something he had no problem with.

Kelly crouched. She ran the marshal's thumb over the bottom of the screen. "But I still want to see if there's anything on it."

He turned again and surveyed the area to make sure no one was around. The two deer had wandered out of sight now.

He couldn't get that dream out of his head.

But how did he tell her he thought he might be suffering from a serious condition? Seeing double...or not. He had no idea.

He needed to see a doctor—for a medical condition or a psychological one. Either way he was sure he would end up with a diagnosis. Why else would he have dreamed of staring at himself on the plane when it was going down?

Maybe it was one of those experiences some people had where they were suddenly watching themselves, like a type of dissociation.

Whichever way he theorized, it wasn't good. But he also wouldn't let it stop him from getting out of here.

No matter what lay at the end of that road.

The back of his neck prickled. He turned to scan the trees around them, watching carefully. Not wanting to be caught unawares.

"You should see this." He heard her shift but didn't turn to look. "It's a bunch of text messages from yesterday and the last few days."

"Does it mention me?"

"They're talking about 'the twins' like that's who they're protecting. But maybe it's code, since the rest of it is pretty cagey."

He blinked, his mind going back again to that dream. "Twins."

"I know, right?" She came over to him. "You never said anything to me about having a brother."

He was sure now. "I do have a brother."

"So there's another one of you out here in the woods—"

"We have company." He tugged on her arm and crouched, all his focus on the man who had come into view about a quarter mile away through the trees.

Thankfully she didn't fight him too much. He whispered, "We need to get out of here."

She shoved the phone under the dead man's body. "Let's go."

"But where? They could see us run, and we'll only get shot in the back."

"It's better than sticking around and getting

shot. I'd rather take my chances." She unclipped Nico's leash. "Come."

The order was clearly meant for the dog, but he couldn't help bristling. "I can take care of myself."

It seemed he'd said that before. Maybe many times. Pleading his case to someone. His brother? "We should go to the crash site. See if he's there."

"Good idea. So let's go." She tugged on his arm.

He pushed up from the crouch, kept his head low and ran after her. Away from the gunmen tracking them. Hunting them.

Toward he didn't know what.

SIX

Nico kept a steady pace while Kelly and even Brett struggled to keep up. Mile after mile they trudged in the direction of the smoke she'd seen yesterday. *Twins.*

She could add that to the list of things Brett hadn't bothered to tell her.

Not that he had to offer her full disclosure when they'd only been colleagues. But the fact was, they were in a situation where they needed to trust each other. Then and now. She wasn't going to harangue him for what he didn't remember at this point. It was hardly his fault that he had some form of amnesia—as bizarre as that sounded.

Still, he'd kept so much from her. Not to mention how he'd gotten her kicked off the case and set her career back years as a result right before he supposedly died. All of it didn't make her feel great.

Kelly wasn't the kind of woman who needed

her ego stroked all the time. But a little bit of respect and trust. A little bit of confidence in herself? That wasn't too much to ask. Was it?

She had fought tooth and nail to get everything she had—not only in her life, but also in her career. With one decision, Brett nearly destroyed everything she'd worked for. There had to be a reason. But she couldn't ask him because he didn't remember. Still, she needed to hope that there was a solid cause behind what he'd done. Maybe the federal case itself.

Though why she would need to be cut out of that was a mystery to her. They could've both finished the case and testified. Why did she need to be ousted?

His voice emerged like a roll of thunder. "Do we know for sure it was talking about me in that text?"

She'd never heard him talk in that low, graveled tone. "What do you mean?"

She could make all the supposition she wanted. The fact was, she had no idea. He was the one who needed to remember enough to give her answers to her questions. More importantly, he needed to testify at the federal case, which made all her hurt feelings so not the point right now.

He kept pace with her. As though he needed the solidarity of her being beside him. "Twins.

It certainly makes my dream a whole lot more rational. Not what I was thinking."

"So you saw your twin in your dream?"

"He told me to strap in because the plane was going down."

"Anything else?" This whole plane crash made no sense. Even if it had been completely accidental, it was a serious fluke that Brett ended up right in the exact place she was. Where the bad guys seemed to know exactly who she was, and now they were targeting both of them.

He shrugged. "My head still hurts, even though I've stopped trying to remember everything."

She winced. "Sorry we didn't get out of here yet. You should've been in a hospital bed yesterday, and we're still walking around in the middle of nowhere."

She didn't add that they had no idea where they were. Although he knew as well as she did that all they had to guide them was the sun's position in the sky and the direction the smoke had been yesterday. Eventually they would find help. They had to because there were no doubt law enforcement officers crawling all over these woods.

"I'd love to find a friendly face." She realized the only one they'd seen so far was that deputy marshal who had been murdered.

"I'd love to find a face that looks exactly like mine."

She reached over and squeezed his forearm. "We will."

She was prepared to support him if he wanted to concentrate on finding his brother before he left these woods and headed to the hospital. Just so long as he was capable. Allowing an injured man to walk farther than he should only made the situation worse in the end.

The next time they came across a group of O'Callaghan's guys they might not be able to run away as fast as they had before.

The next time could be the last.

It seemed selfish to grieve that her life was in jeopardy, but all she'd been focused on for the past two years since the undercover case was her police career. And more recently, she'd been securing a foothold on the police K-9 team since she got Nico. She would lose everything.

Again.

But the course of justice against the O'Callaghans was on the line. She of all people wanted them taken down. The destruction that organized crime family had caused all over Chicago was unbelievable.

Nico perked up.

"What is it, dog?" When it was only the two of them out here for hours on end, of course she talked to Nico as though her partner understood everything she said, rather than just the portion Nico knew of the couple of hundred words that she could learn. They were more in tune with each other's mannerisms and body language.

"Do you think she found another person?"

Kelly realized again as she shrugged that both of them had taken everything that happened so far in stride. Except for her freak-out about her hands, and his about the phone. Her palms felt a lot better now, the skin not quite so painful— or at least that was what she was telling herself. "I guess we'll find out."

Someone had already lost a husband or father. Or son. There was a dead man out here, and in another place there was a person whose world was about to be turned upside down.

"There it is." His pace quickened.

Now she knew what Nico had sniffed. The tang of smoke laced the air where there should've been a commotion. Flashing lights or floodlights set up. People all around, uniforms and technicians collecting evidence. Cops and federal agents.

She saw no one.

Kelly tugged on the sleeve of his T-shirt. "Not so fast. I want to check out the area and make sure it's safe before we just go rushing over to the plane."

From what she could see he didn't like it, but he also didn't argue. He slowed, and they both studied the wreckage. He pushed out a harsh breath. "I seriously survived that?"

"Someone was looking out for you." And she was happy to give God all the credit for saving his life. If the Lord wanted this federal case to go ahead and justice to be served, then that would happen. She didn't need to doubt that He was sovereign.

All she had to do was trust what He wanted to do in her life.

She winced. As though it was that easy.

He said, "Where is Brett?"

Okay, there was something wrong with him. Kelly turned. "You're Brett."

He shook his head. "I'm not Brett. I'm Ethan."

He stumbled back a step and nearly went down. Kelly caught his elbows.

"Ethan?" She sounded as confused as he was.

He nodded. Everything in him was more than certain. In a way he knew he'd said that many times over the course of his life, probably when people mistook him for his brother.

His brother.

He blinked. They were the twins. Brett and Ethan.

"You're not the one testifying. Brett is." She

wore the same expression, but he couldn't help thinking her words meant he wasn't the one who needed protecting. Or rescuing. If she wanted to, she could leave him here and find his brother instead. Be the hero who delivered the witness to the federal agents in charge of his protection.

"Do you remember anything else?"

He shrugged out of her hold. "I want to walk around the wreckage and see if anyone else survived."

"And I want you to do that. You might remember even more, maybe everything."

He knew there were things he wouldn't like.

"But first we need to make sure the area is secure. This place should be crawling with cops, and yet it's empty of people." She bit her lip.

"They could have shown up while I wasn't here." There could be people searching for him right now. But if that was true, why hadn't they found him? "Isn't that why you were looking for me?"

"I was trying to find the plane. No one knew where it had crashed, even though we heard the Mayday call over the radio. I was only looking for marshals and their witness. I had no idea it was Brett, or that you were out here as well."

"Okay," he agreed. "Let's observe first before we rush in. I for one don't want to get shot."

"Let's hunker down over there." She waved to a tree, then turned to her dog.

He didn't hear the words she spoke, just the high tone. Her voice sounded excited, and Nico began to bound around, moving from side to side in a jump. Bending her shoulders to the ground so that her front legs were outstretched for a second, Nico shook her whole body and then sat.

"Nico, search." Kelly pointed, then turned to watch as her partner bounded down the trail toward the airplane wreckage.

Ethan had a flash of something that came out of nowhere. In his mind he saw the handheld device. On screen was the dog's-eye view of the interior of a building. The animal had been attached to his squad in the Marines. The meanest Belgian Malinois he'd ever seen in his life. Until one time he'd been holding a chicken sandwich.

After that, the dog was his best friend.

Two days later their squad got hit in the town square, pinned down by rebels until they had to call in air support for rescue. No one in the village had survived. And in the end, they'd carried out three of his friends and the dog—whose stubbornness meant he survived two surgeries and all the physical therapy it took for him to get back to being a dog. Just not a marine.

Ethan muttered to himself. "What was his name?"

"What was that?" Kelly asked.

"There was a dog in my unit. I can't remember his name, though." Ethan shook his head. That didn't make it feel any better. "Is Nico—"

"Here she comes."

Ethan said, "What does it mean that she's headed back here?"

"If she didn't bark when she was out of sight, then she didn't find anyone."

He felt his brows rise. "She didn't see anyone at all?"

Kelly said, "She would've alerted us if she had."

She crouched and dug in the backpack for that same yellow ball. The one he remembered was as much of a treat for the dog in his unit as any food would be. Kelly rewarded Nico in the same way, letting her catch the ball a couple of times before she clicked her tongue. "Come on, let's go."

Ethan followed her toward the plane crash. Most of the small aircraft was intact, except one of the wings had been torn off and the tail was missing a section from the top. He headed straight for the door on the side of the plane, open likely because people had exited that way to get off. Him being one of them. Unless of course it was open because it had popped open during the crash.

He wished he remembered how the plane had come down.

And why.

He needed this whole thing to jog his memory. Instead of forcing it, Ethan decided to simply look around and allow the memories to come on their own.

He stepped inside the airplane. Panels had detached from the ceiling, and oxygen masks hung on their tubing. He walked down the aisle and saw several backpacks. A laptop bag. No people. Ethan turned and headed for the cockpit, where a uniformed man slumped over the controls.

He didn't need to press two fingers to the man's neck to know the pilot was dead.

"Anything?"

He realized Kelly had remained right behind him. "Shouldn't Nico have alerted about this guy?"

"She already found one guy today. All I needed from her was to know if there was a threat, and she didn't indicate there was."

He lifted both hands.

"Sorry, I shouldn't yell at you." She sighed. "It's really bizarre there's no one here, and I have no idea what we're supposed to do next."

She glanced at the dead pilot. "Is there any way to tell if the radio is working?"

Ethan glanced around the plane. "Maybe I can find another phone in one of these bags. Get some answers about why no one is here."

She nodded. "Be careful." She seemed adamant about that despite the fact she'd been essentially yelling at him just now.

Then again, maybe he preferred her way of expressing frustration. Considering how his brother was, it almost comforted him to know that there was someone capable of being honest about their feelings. Or what they were thinking.

Kelly didn't hide much of anything. He knew she didn't want to upset him, and she hadn't pestered him with questions he couldn't answer.

His brother was out here somewhere. "I'm happy to call for help, but I want to be out looking for Brett as soon as it comes."

"I can't believe I thought you were him." She shook her head. "Now that I know the truth, it's obvious why you seem so different from him."

"Thank you."

Ethan didn't know why he said that, or what it indicated had been between him and his brother recently. Or for their entire lives.

She knew Brett. Maybe better than Ethan did,

considering how much time he and his brother had spent apart.

He frowned and searched a couple of bags, coming up empty. Why did he think there was contention between him and Brett? Maybe it was outright bad blood.

Being in the airplane again hadn't brought anything back. He knew his name but nothing else about his life or what'd happened.

"I found a laptop." He pulled it out and handed it over, just in case it was helpful to her.

Nico wandered around the interior of the airplane.

The dog came over to him, sniffed the side of his head and licked his ear.

"Did you find anything, girl?" Ethan scratched her side. He rummaged in the backpack and found more personal belongings. A couple of books and what looked like FBI files that probably shouldn't have been left behind.

In the bottom of the backpack was a flip phone.

"Huh."

Kelly said, "What is it?"

"This." He flipped the phone open. "It's switched off, but I'll see if it has any signal."

"Probably a burner phone."

"It was at the bottom of the backpack. Buried like someone didn't want it to be found." He

checked the bars as soon as it booted up, then
handed the phone to Kelly. "Care to do the—"

A man stood in the doorway.

He swung up a gun, intent in his eyes.

Before the guy could squeeze the trigger,
Ethan drew the gun from his waistband and
fired.

SEVEN

The blast of her gun going off filled the interior of the airplane. Kelly felt her body jerk. There was a split second where she wondered if she'd been shot, but the one holding the gun was Ethan.

Not Brett. His twin brother.

She could hardly assimilate what was going on as fast as it was happening. And there was no time yet again. She twisted to look where he had fired but saw nothing in the doorway of the airplane.

She turned back to him.

"There was a guy. He was going to shoot you." The intent in his eyes was something she had seen on the faces of cops before. A man accustomed to having to do what was necessary to save his own life and the life of people with him. Which, for a former marine, was not surprising.

"Then you saved my life. And Nico's."

It didn't mean she completely trusted him, but she didn't have a choice with the state of her hands.

"Police! Put the gun down." She recognized the voice. Even above the ringing in her ears she knew it was her boss, the chief of the police department. "Put it down now!"

But it sounded like backup was finally here. The US Marshals could protect Ethan, and she could head out to search for Brett the way she and Nico had trained to do.

Kelly knew whoever was out there would take care of the situation. "Look around some more. I need something of Brett's if you want Nico to search for him out here."

Ethan's brother could already be under police protection or at the hospital. He could also be out in the woods, lost the way Ethan had been. She knew just how badly Ethan wanted to find his brother when he nodded and got to work.

"Stop! Police!" Her chief sounded furious.

Nico leaned against her leg and whined. Kelly reached down and rubbed the dog's head.

Ethan said, "I have a sweater here that Brett wears all the time."

Good. "You should put that on so you can get warm and find me something else."

"Like a pair of socks?"

"Worn is better than clean," Kelly said.

"Oh-kay."

She didn't get into an explanation. "Bring it all with you but stay behind me." Kelly moved to the doorway. Nico went ahead of her and stepped into view of the people outside. She reached to pull the dog back when someone spoke.

"Officer Wayne!" It was her chief. "You in there?"

"Yes, sir!" She remembered Ethan's reaction to her calling in backup and glanced at him. He might not recall why he'd felt the need to hide his presence from the police or the marshals, and she wanted to get a read on him now.

His face had paled. *Not good.*

Kelly wasn't going to lie about him being on the plane. She was, however, going to get a feel for the situation first.

"I'm coming out," she called to the door. Then to Ethan she said, "Come out when you're ready. When you think it's safe."

She would allow Ethan to decide when he wanted to make his presence known. She figured that at least meant she got a chance to see who was out there first.

"I'm pretty sure safe means sticking with you," he muttered back to her.

She shot him a smile. "I could say the same about you."

He might be the target here as much as his brother was, if only to provide leverage the O'Callaghans could use against Brett. But Ethan was by no means a victim. No more than she was.

"Nico, heel." She stepped out. Nico hopped clear of the door and they crossed to her chief and a US marshal. "What happened to the guy from the plane doorway?"

The chief said, "Ran off into the woods."

Douglas Filburn was in his fifties but still fit. The chief went to spin class with his wife every Friday—her idea. And it showed, even though he always ate a giant meatball sandwich for lunch on those days.

Beside him was a shorter, stocky man. Everything about him was gray, as though he had been carved from stone. Except for the bandage on his forehead, which was tinged with pink in the middle. A deputy US marshal who had been injured in the crash.

Hopefully they wouldn't ask her if anyone was inside.

"Sir." She nodded to the chief.

He said, "This is Officer Wayne and her K-9."

The granite man stuck out his hand. "Deputy Marshal Cliff Edmonton."

She shook hands with him. "Has the witness been located?"

The chief shook his head. "We believe he was with the man you found shot to the east of here. Why didn't you call in?"

"I've been out here all night. One of O'Callaghan's guys tossed my sat phone in the river and my cell phone died. That's why I had to call in from the marshal's phone."

Edmonton nodded. "We're glad you did. When I woke up after the crash, the witness and the marshal were gone. Along with another member of our party."

"Is there any way to figure out why the plane crashed?" Maybe the deputy could tell them since he'd been on the plane, and, unlike Ethan, seemed to remember who he was. Hopefully any information he could give would help Ethan get his memories back.

Now she knew he wasn't Brett, it wasn't hard to see him differently, or to view the parts of him that intrigued her as things that set him apart from other men she had met.

Relationships weren't something she'd thought she had time for. Not after the way her dad never got over her mother's death or how so many guys still viewed female cops. Brett had just tossed her off the case like she wasn't even good enough to be his colleague—let alone a friend.

Now Ethan came along and challenged everything she'd thought.

She'd never even been attracted to Brett. It hadn't crossed her mind, and she doubted it ever would have even if they'd had the chance to get to know each other better.

Ethan was just different. In two days he'd been more of a partner to her than anyone else in her life.

Except Nico.

Their attention drifted past her to the plane. Hoping it wasn't another vicious armed man, she spun around.

The chief would at some point figure out she'd hurt her hands. He would wonder how she'd managed to fire that shot. She would have to tell him the truth. It would come with the paperwork. The after-action reports. The blow of justice to the O'Callaghan family when the judge brought the sentence down on Michael and he could no longer walk free.

Ethan walked toward them from the plane. The marshal went to meet him halfway, and they shook hands.

The chief said, "Is that Brett?"

She realized Filburn was asking her. "This is Brett's twin brother Ethan. I found him in the woods." They'd saved each other's lives. But they hadn't found the witness.

She studied the dark look in Filburn's eyes and the way his brows drew together. He wasn't happy at all. "You really do know these people, then."

Kelly said, "I had no idea Brett Harrigan was the one testifying."

"The real question is why did this plane crash here." Filburn folded his arms across his expansive chest.

Kelly nodded. "I was wondering the same thing."

The chief pinned her with a look. "Did the men O'Callaghan sent here see your face at any point in the last two days?"

She froze. "Chief, you know I was involved with the case?"

"What's this?" Ethan moved to stand beside Kelly. Nico was on her other side, leaning against her leg. He rounded out the solidarity.

"I'd like to know the same thing," Deputy Marshal Edmonton said.

Kelly shifted and the outside of her arm brushed his. As though she needed that brief moment of solidarity so she could say, "Chief Filburn, why did you just ask me if any of O'Callaghan's men saw my face?"

Ethan figured it was because the older man knew she had been undercover in the past. Was she not aware he had known?

Filburn said, "You think I hired you without calling Chicago and asking about your history?"

"My name was never listed on any paperwork attached to that case. Neither was Brett's, which means no one who wasn't privy to the investigation—which was maybe three cops, one of whom was the commissioner, plus my dad—should have any idea I was ever undercover with the O'Callaghans."

The marshal gasped. "You're the one."

Ethan and Kelly both turned to Edmonton. She chuckled, but it contained no humor. "I'm beginning to think everyone here knows something I don't."

Ethan spun to her. "Not me." At least, not that he could remember.

His head sent a surge of pain rolling through his skull. He hissed out a breath and lifted his hand to touch the side of his head while he breathed through it.

Kelly touched his elbow. "Ethan, you need to see a doctor."

"Good idea," her chief said. "Officer Wayne, accompany Mr. Harrigan to the hospital, and I'll make sure uniforms escort you all the way there."

Kelly folded her arms.

"Who is it you're trying to protect?" Ethan

asked. "Me, or her?" He motioned with his thumb over his shoulder.

"Doesn't matter. The two of you stay together, and that's not up for debate."

The marshal nodded. "Sounds like a good idea to me."

"Really?" Kelly said. "Because I don't think you have another K-9 handler who can work Nico on a scent search until she finds Brett Harrigan. Or do you know something else I don't?"

Her chief worked his jaw side to side but said nothing.

"Your dog can find my witness?" The deputy marshal's eyebrows rose.

Ethan didn't know if he was supposed to trust this guy or not. The plane had come down suddenly, beeping sensors one moment and a crash the next. It was just enough time for Brett to get buckled in, and then they were dropping from the sky.

But had it been planned, or was this a mechanical failure? Given how quickly O'Callaghan's men had swarmed the general location, and how the Marshals Service seemed absent, someone might have sabotaged the airplane and delivered Brett and Ethan right into their hands.

And maybe Kelly as well, considering she had been undercover with Brett.

They needed a lot more information if they were going to keep each other safe.

He realized then that was exactly what he wanted to do. Rather than go back into the custody of the US Marshals, a bunch of people who were professional and highly capable but who he didn't know, he wanted to be with her. He'd spent two days with Kelly and had seen something of how deep she ran. He could get to know her more and they'd take care of one another.

Preferably while they found Brett.

The chief groaned. Kelly spun to the marshal. "Yes, we have an item of clothing that belongs to Brett for Nico to get a scent. There's no one in this county qualified to do it except me. Nico and I can find him."

He wanted her to say that she wouldn't do it without Ethan going as well, but his head began to pound again. The sensation rose until it felt like his skull was splitting open.

He turned away from them, walked a few steps and tried to breathe through it.

"How soon can we get transport here to take Ethan to the hospital?"

So she was going to cart him off to see a doctor while she traipsed around these woods alone? Sure, she was a capable police officer. But without backup? He wasn't about to be trapped at the mercy of medical professionals knowing she was out here.

"I'm going with you."

"You can't even see straight." She shook her head. "How are you going to walk miles?"

"I'm going." He just needed to swallow down the feeling of being sick. And get his balance back.

She handed him one of her water bottles. "You need to see a doctor."

"And I need to find my witness," Deputy Marshal Edmonton said.

The feeling of being nothing but a pawn shuffled between people rose in him. So familiar he knew it wasn't unusual that he felt this way. Ethan didn't like it now any more than he had previously. When his parents shuffled them between Mom and Dad as often as they liked. When Brett dragged him into witness protection just because they shared a face, not caring that Ethan had his own life to live.

But what kind of life was it?

He didn't even know where he lived or what he did.

At the same time, distant memories had begun to work their way back into his consciousness.

"No one who is being hunted is walking around these woods." Chief Filburn glanced at the deputy marshal. "Even for the chance to find the witness, it's not worth the risk."

"To your people." The deputy made a face.

"And you care nothing for the brother of your witness? You're just going to let him walk around these woods trying to find Brett?"

"Actually," the deputy marshal said, "I figure he's about to pass out. All I have to do is get him to the hospital and then I can protect your officer while she finds my witness."

"How about instead of him passing out, we get Ethan to a car or something?" Kelly made the same move she'd done in the river. She held his weight under his shoulder, supporting him as they moved.

The pain eclipsed everything, and he couldn't see the terrain in front of his feet. But he knew she was there. Helping him with every step. Vulnerable, yet strong. Beautiful and caring.

"Easy," she said. "We'll get there."

Ethan wanted to know if she really was going to look for his brother when these gunmen knew who she was. He figured she would absolutely do it, whether she had backup or not. Maybe her chief was right to be nervous. It could be she cared about Brett more than he realized, and the idea of getting to know her better was nothing but a dream.

One full of shooters and running.

In the end, Ethan would have to watch his brother walk away with everything he wanted.

"I got him." The marshal took over from her. "I'll take him to the hospital. You guys should meet me there so we can plan how to find Brett."

Ethan felt the seat under him and was shuffled into the back.

The engine turned on.

Ethan hissed at the rumble under his cheek. He couldn't even open his eyes, let alone speak.

"And when I find him," the deputy mumbled, "I'm going to finish the job and kill him."

EIGHT

Kelly followed the chief to his car parked beside the marshal's vehicle. The fed pulled out so fast his tires kicked up dust.

She pulled the rear door open. "In."

Nico hopped onto the back seat and lay down. Kelly got in the front, managed to buckle her seat belt and let out a long breath. Part of her didn't want to relax even though she was safe now.

The chief pulled out, following the marshal.

Ethan was protected, and he would get medical care. She could go back to her job and her life. It was entirely possible they weren't going to see each other again—especially not if he went back to witness protection with Brett after the trial.

Nico groaned and stretched out on the back seat.

Kelly glanced back at her. *I know how you feel.* She should be grateful for the reprieve, not thinking how her boss should have a K-9 rear compartment in his car.

She'd kept the entirety of the dog training to herself so none of them were inconvenienced by what she wanted to accomplish here. They were more likely to agree to her being a permanent part of the department if it only made their jobs easier, and the PD as a whole better. Something the community saw as a positive addition.

The chief glanced over. "You okay?" He lowered his chin and motioned to her hands.

She lifted her palms. Both bandages were dirty, and the abrasions likely needed cleaning. "We made do with what we had."

"Let's get you to the hospital as well. Have the doctors check you out."

He probably figured there was more she hadn't said. Because Kelly never told him more than what he absolutely needed to know. Call it a throwback to what Brett had done, but she didn't like being vulnerable. Or putting her trust in people she didn't know she could implicitly rely on.

Chief Filburn seemed like a good guy, and he was a solid cop. Time would tell on all that. But if he turned down her and the K-9 attachment to his department it was a moot point.

The marshal's car was a quarter mile up ahead, where Ethan lay in the back seat. They turned on to the highway and immediately sped up.

Kelly frowned. "What is—"

The chief didn't let her finish. "Maybe there's a problem." Filburn flipped on his lights and sirens. "We'll escort them. Get their protectee the help he needs."

"His name is Ethan. He's the witness's twin brother." She wasn't telling him anything he didn't already know. Apparently. "The O'Callaghans know that, so he's in as much danger as Brett."

"And you."

There was an odd tone in his voice. Kelly made sure Nico was all right as they sped down the highway. The dog was not quite asleep, as though she didn't want to lose her awareness of what was happening around her. Kelly didn't blame her. She had good instincts.

The car in front went even faster, and the deputy marshal changed lanes erratically.

Kelly frowned. "What is he doing?"

Maybe the chief was right, and Ethan had suffered a turn for the worse in the back of the car. Good thing they were following. Two cars were better than one, making a convoy to get to the hospital where they were supposed to regroup.

Filburn said, "We're not going to address the fact you're in as much danger as the twins are?" He didn't waste a second adding, "And without the marshals to protect you."

She frowned. "I'm not the one testifying. Unless you're secretly working for the O'Callaghans, I'm not currently in danger."

"You think I'd have looked out for you all this time if I was?"

Kelly twisted in her seat. She had to take her attention from the car hurtling along the highway up ahead, and the chief struggling to keep pace, but what he'd just said was too much. "Looking out for me?"

"That's what I said." He was completely unapologetic. "Stipulation when I hired you. Came with your personnel file. A note that said you had a serious threat against you, listed in your file. The O'Callaghan family knows who you are. Michael O'Callaghan knows you're a cop. It's why you got the job with my department all the way out here."

Kelly felt the world spin around her, while she struggled to retain a hold on everything she knew. "I was kicked off that undercover case because they *made* me?" She shook her head. "That makes no sense at all. I'd have been told."

Filburn shrugged. "It was high-level. Someone made the decision to cut you loose, and it worked if you think about it. You're alive, aren't you?"

"And you know," she said. "And it's why I got a job all the way out here."

"No one else would hire you, right?"

"I got a couple of rejections, sure. Police departments that wouldn't have had the budget for a K-9 unit anyway." She frowned. "You're saying someone put me with you?"

She'd thought it was God moving in her life, the way a spot opened up in the town where her dad lived. A way to keep an eye on him.

Filburn shrugged. "I knew your dad in the service years ago. I owed him a favor. So when he called me, I let the other departments know I wanted to hire you. They helped me point you in the right direction."

"Why?" She needed to hear him say it out loud.

"Because your father asked me to keep you safe from the O'Callaghans. Head down. Off the radar." He frowned. "Now they're crawling all over my county. We're going to have to stash you somewhere they won't find you."

Kelly didn't know where to start. "How did my father get the idea I was a target?" He couldn't possibly have known she'd been made. Even *she* didn't know.

She'd been shoved off the case, thanks to Brett Harrigan. No one had mentioned to Kelly that she was in danger or that the O'Callaghans knew who she was. Now she'd overheard that conversation from inside the cave she was inclined to believe it.

The chief said, "Someone called to warn your dad you could be in danger if you got close to them again."

"Close? I was undercover in their family." Until Brett got her kicked off the case.

"Guess they really did figure out you're a cop."

Her stomach did a flip. The chief was still going pretty fast. When he changed lanes at high speed it didn't help. "This is unbelievable. If I was made, I'd have been told. If I was in danger every day since then, so that I needed a job under the radar where the O'Callaghans couldn't find me, surely someone would actually have told… I don't know, *me*?"

"Your dad wanted you to have a clean break."

"So I could get killed because I had no idea? That's a great plan."

"We kept you safe," Filburn said. "The family had no idea where you were."

Kelly wanted to run her hands down her face, but it would be far too painful. She dug her cell phone out of the backpack, pushing Brett's socks down into her things, which would taint the scent.

She let out a hiss. This whole situation had gone haywire.

She used the chief's phone charger to plug in her cell. As soon as she had enough juice, she would get information from her dad. Otherwise what else could she believe about the last two years since that undercover case?

"What is he doing?" the chief muttered.

The car in front nearly hit another car but kept going.

"Get closer." Kelly leaned forward to peer at what looked like Ethan, now sitting up. Then the car swerved.

She gasped. It careened to the shoulder, cut off a truck and camping trailer and kept going. Over the rumble strip and up an embankment.

The chief hit the brakes, and Kelly held on as they headed after it.

But there was nothing they could do.

The car hit a dip, the front end rushed up out of it and the car flipped over.

Ethan hissed out a breath and reached for his rifle. It was nowhere to be found. His head pounded and his vision swam, but he knew who he was. Until he opened his eyes.

No uniform. No weapon. He was crumpled on the roof of a car, lying upside down on the grass. Not in Afghanistan. The vehicle was on its roof, but not because of an IED.

His friends.

Brett.

Past and present mixed like someone stuffed his mind in a dryer and the thing swirled around and around. Was it going to stop at some point?

He didn't know where he was. A state park? Wilderness somewhere chilly enough the cold air cut through Brett's sweater and made him shiver despite the trickle of sweat that ran down his face.

He lifted the hem of the T-shirt that was far too large and swiped his forehead. *Ouch.* That didn't feel good. And now the material had a soaking of blood on it.

Not the first time he'd been hurt and likely not the last.

That was about the most his brain could come up with. Random thoughts. The odd idea. But getting his arms and legs to move? Not so much. That part of his brain seemed to be having some trouble communicating.

The way Alice inferred he was deficient. *Guess it's not just relationships where I'm like that.*

Ethan frowned. It wasn't his fiancé Alice that he'd been hanging out with recently. That relationship had ended years ago. He pictured a blonde woman in hiking clothes and a German shepherd in his mind. Brett. Where was his brother?

Fear trickled into his awareness like the cold could prickle his consciousness with goose bumps in response. He had no idea what he was supposed to be worried about, but there was something. He'd just have to remember what it was.

A shuffle from the front seat drew his attention. Ethan frowned.

Voices penetrated his consciousness—shouts from nearby. The front door opened with a groan of metal and a grunt from whoever sat up there.

He tried to speak. All that emerged from his mouth was a puff of air.

Ethan tried to move. That didn't work either. He was trapped like last time. Like when the plane had come down. How many times had he been in accidents now? He lost count, and everything blurred into one flash of terror. *Kill him.* Someone was in danger.

Was it him?

Where was Brett?

"Are you okay?" The words were muffled and male. He didn't hear the response and couldn't make one of his own. He needed to get out of here. Call for help. Move.

Someone thumped the outside of the car. "This guy tried to kill us!"

Ethan blinked.

"We need to get him out," the first guy said. "Check you're both okay."

His driver said, "Leave him to die for all I care. I can't believe he did that. Just because he wants to go after his brother."

On the far side of the car, a woman's legs came into view beyond his running shoes. A second later, the door was shoved open. "Nico, out."

The nose of a shepherd came into view.

"No, out."

The dog backed up and the woman crawled in. Her eyes widened at the sight of him. She was beautiful, and her presence here was a lifeline he desperately needed. *Lord, I don't like being helpless.* Faith had always felt like a battle to him, a wrestling match between who he was and wanted to be.

Always trying to find peace.

"Hey." She crawled alongside him on the roof, close enough to touch his face. But the touch was rougher than skin, more like bandages.

He thought she might try to move his head one way, then the other, and clasped her elbows.

"Okay, it's okay." She hissed. "That looks nasty."

He tried to hold on but his hands fell back to his lap. That guy, the driver. She needed to know. "Bad."

"What?"

Ethan struggled to form the words. "Bad. Guy."

She frowned and her gaze moved over his face. "Have you ever had a TBI before?"

He couldn't think about that. She had to know they were in danger. What did it matter about his concussions and everything else? His head was a swirl of emotions. Memories of guys in fatigues.

One shouted in his face.

Another shoved him aside.

And then they were running. Gunshots rang around him. Kelly turned back. "Chief! He needs Life Flight."

"They're twenty minutes out!"

Kelly touched Ethan's cheeks again. "Just hang on with me for a bit, okay? I don't think you should pass out or go to sleep."

Mmm. Sleep sounded good. But Ethan didn't want to quit looking at her.

"What happened? It looked like you attacked him, and he says you crashed the car." Her voice was little more than a murmur.

Ethan needed to… He had to… "Kill him."

"You wanted to kill him?"

No, that wasn't right. "Brett."

"You want to kill Brett."

Ethan frowned. It was all he could do. Moving his head wasn't an option.

"He wanted to kill Brett."

He closed his eyes for a second.

"Okay." Her expression softened. "The marshal works for O'Callaghan?"

He blinked again, but that a good and bad given he was fighting unconsciousness. She patted his cheek, and he opened his eyes. Kelly said, "Okay. I've got you, yeah?"

He tried to smile.

She squeezed his shoulder, then turned. "Nico."

The dog came in. Kelly said, "Guard." Then she crawled to the door.

Nico turned and sat beside him. Ethan laid a hand on her back for reassurance. The animal didn't move.

"I'll go with him," she said. "When Life Flight gets here, will you take Nico back to the precinct kennels? I should be at the hospital, too, and it makes no sense to make two trips or go separately."

She planned to stick with him. Unlike Alice.

That made Ethan feel better, even though his mind couldn't collate a couple of thoughts into something that made any sense. And he was fading fast.

No. He wasn't going to go out like that.

Ethan had to move. *Lord, help me.*

He patted the dog twice. Enough the animal got the idea something was happening. Then Ethan shifted. Hands on the roof of the car on either side of his hips, he shuffled his whole body along toward the door.

It was slow going, but he was determined.

Nico moved with him. When he neared the door, Nico shifted to stand between his knees. The dog went first out the door. Ethan couldn't do much more but slide to the frame around the door, his legs on the grass.

"He's coming out!" The marshal reeled back, blood on his face. Looked like he'd broken his nose. "He's working with them. He tried to kill me!"

Nico growled.

"It's okay, dog." Ethan didn't know whether he managed to say the words or not. They were in his mind, but his ears kept ringing.

The marshal drew his weapon. He held it out, not exactly pointing it at Ethan, but the intent was there.

"Whoa—"

The marshal cut her off. "I'm not going to let the O'Callaghans win!"

Ethan braced to get shot.

Nico moved first. Faster than Ethan's vision

could track, the dog raced to the marshal and jumped.

The blast of the gunshot eclipsed everything. His body jerked and he fell back. The dog snarled, and there was a dull thud, the sound of a man screaming. "He's going to kill me!"

And then everything went black.

NINE

Chief Filburn stepped on the marshal's wrist, then kicked away the gun. Kelly motioned to Nico, who lifted her paws from the guy's chest and returned to her side.

"My dog isn't going to kill you. He just knocked you off-balance." The way the marshal had with his words about Ethan. And the way Ethan had been knocked back even though the shot went wide.

She wanted to go back to where Ethan now lay, but it wasn't like she could help him. She could just make sure he wasn't hurt more than he'd already been. "You said twenty minutes on the Life Flight helicopter, Chief?"

He nodded, that experienced gaze dark on her.

"You sicced your dog on me," Edmonton gasped.

Kelly figured he'd know what was happening if she *actually* did. Nico had some protection training. She could take down a suspect. It was also something they'd never used in real life, only in training. She knew what Nico was capable of. She hadn't needed to put that strength and determination into action before.

The chief cuffed the marshal's hands behind his back and hauled the guy off the ground. "Care to explain what that was?"

The marshal just glared at her.

Kelly said, "I'm guessing Nico recognized something in the marshal, and she didn't like it. Considering he was holding a gun on a man he's supposed to be protecting, I think she did right."

Chief Filburn said, "So we believe the guy we don't know and distrust the agent?"

Honestly? Yes, that was exactly the way Kelly leaned. Call it instinct or something else.

"At the least, he can't make accusations without cause." She needed to make sure Ethan was okay, but turned to the marshal and said, "What evidence do you have that Mr. Harrigan is somehow compromised?"

They had no idea what brought the plane down, and this man could tell them. He might even know where to find Brett.

The chief moved the marshal to the front end of the car. "Talk."

Kelly motioned for Nico to lie down and went

to check on Ethan. She touched his face. Why did she keep doing that? She'd never had the urge to do it with Brett. That would've been weird. But with Ethan, things were different.

There was no room in her life for a relationship. Her career had to take precedent until things were settled with the K-9 unit here.

Now that it was clear there was more to her life than what she'd known about her taking this job, she needed to clear that up before she could even think about anything else. Or figure out what her future looked like.

Ethan was out cold. He'd been through the wringer and needed to get to the hospital. Thankfully the helicopter was almost there.

"He okay?" the chief called out.

"His head, and he passed out which can't be good." She backed up to stand and zeroed her gaze in on the marshal. "Why did the plane go down?"

Edmonton huffed out a breath.

"You think you're not gonna talk? You're in our county now," she said. "That means, whether you like it or not, that witness is getting to his court appearance. Justice happens here, and that includes the times when everything and everyone is against it. Or when it's our job to solve the murder of a US marshal who was your colleague. No matter who killed him."

"You think I'm some kind of dirty fed? Like I took a bribe?" Edmonton huffed out a laugh.

She shrugged. "Maybe you're only acting under duress. We won't know unless you talk. Which you will, in case you didn't get that."

The sound of a helicopter in the distance registered. Good. They needed to get Ethan to the hospital.

Kelly said, "I was police in Chicago. And I can tell you, we don't do corruption here."

Chief Filburn's expression shifted. "As much as I don't like the idea of disbelieving another cop, if there's suspicion, I'm not letting you go yet. You're in our custody, Deputy Marshal Edmonton, until I get an explanation."

"How about the fact that guy is the one who crashed the car?" the marshal said. "He tried to kill both of us. And for what?"

Ethan had told her the marshal was a bad guy. If she'd have let him, Edmonton might've killed him.

Kelly folded her arms. "When he's awake, I'll ask."

And she would believe Ethan's word before this guy's. Even if it wasn't the best idea to do so without evidence to back it up, her instincts screamed at her that Ethan was the one to believe. There was something this marshal wasn't saying.

Had he killed his fellow deputy in the woods and lost Brett? Maybe Brett was already dead.

"If you won't say how the plane went down," the chief said, "how about telling us where Brett Harrigan is?"

"I told you they were all gone when I woke up."

Edmonton might've said more but the chopper closed in on them. She wanted to ask how many marshals had been on that plane. They were flying blind, as it were, given Ethan had suffered amnesia, and she wasn't sure she believed a word this guy said.

The wind whipped up, and the sound grew until she couldn't hear anything else. She shaded her eyes from the swirling dust and watched as they landed.

Two EMTs rushed over with their gear.

Kelly pointed to Ethan as the first one reached her. "He had a head injury, and he was slurring his words pretty badly." She leaned in. "Now he's unconscious."

They got to work, and Ethan was loaded onto a yellow board.

She wanted to go with him. Instead, she held herself still—Nico leaning against her leg—while the chopper flew off. Then she turned to the chief. "I want to be at the hospital when he wakes up."

The chief nodded. "I'll have an officer meet the chopper at the other end to watch over him."

Kelly moved in front of the marshal, determined to get an answer. "Where is Brett Harrigan?"

Edmonton said, "Lost in the woods."

"How long have you been under the thumb of the O'Callaghans?"

He flinched. "You think justice is that simple? Like you do the right thing, and everything is perfect?"

"I know that's not how it works." Though Kelly would do the best she could in the context of the whole system. "I'm not naive just because I'm a woman."

"You have no clue what's going on here. You think your department can do anything about the O'Callaghan family?" The marshal huffed out a breath. "You're all out of your league."

"Maybe. But Ethan will remain safe, and we'll find Brett."

They better not have killed him. She prayed then, admitting she needed God to keep Brett alive until they could find him. He might be lost and hurt, alone in the woods. On the run from guys with guns.

Nico had the skills to track him, and Kelly had a contaminated sample. Still, she was going to try.

Ideally, she'd have Brett there with her when Ethan woke up. God could do that. It would certainly be His work, and not because of her.

The marshal smirked. If it was anyone but the chief with her she'd tell him to take the guy away. She was done talking to him, and had no interest in trying to force more out of Edmonton. In fact, the chief could do that if he wanted.

It was time for Nico to work.

The chief loaded the marshal in the back of his car, then turned to her before she could get in the front passenger seat. "Officer Wayne."

"Yes, chief?"

"I don't want you going off by yourself. Not without backup."

Kelly didn't like the sound of that. "Nico and I can—"

"It's not up for debate," the chief said. "See a doctor. Question Ethan. Don't go anywhere without backup until further notice. Understood?"

Kelly nodded, not liking this at all. "Yes, Chief."

It seemed like an hour before the doctor came into his hospital room but was probably more like twenty minutes. Ethan shifted on the bed and tried to sit up. He caught a glance of the uniformed police officer at the door.

Was he being protected or contained?

"Whoa there." The doctor lifted a hand, palm out. "Take it easy, okay?" He eyed Ethan in a way that made Ethan wonder who the guy thought he was. Or what the police or the marshals had told him. If there were any marshals in the hospital.

Probably the doctor didn't have any clue Ethan was enrolled in witness security.

Ethan said, "I'm good."

The doctor showed him the button to raise the back of his bed. "I highly doubt that's true."

I'm not lying. Ethan waited until the thing was a little more upright before he thought about speaking. Mostly because he had to contain nausea that swirled up to his throat. He'd said those words to Kelly.

An image of her swam in his mind. Trying to help him. Believing him when he told her that marshal was dirty. Where was she now? He didn't even know how long it had been since he passed out. Just that he'd regained consciousness in the helicopter and been awake all through the travel, then the long tests and answering a million questions.

Where was she?

The doctor said, "How about I start from the beginning?"

Ethan nodded.

"The tests indicate you have a mild concussion, though I always hesitate to use the qualifier of 'mild.' Especially in the case of someone who I suspect has had previous head injuries and presents with measurable memory loss."

"You have my medical history?" Ethan would be surprised if anyone gave the doctor access to it. He could barely remember his own name, let alone the identification he was supposed to give out. The fake name the US marshals had given him.

The doctor frowned. "No, and I would love to see it."

"I've had concussions before. This one doesn't seem as bad." Except for the whole not-remembering-his-name thing.

"I'm going to reserve judgment on that. Sometimes symptoms can crop up later rather than immediately. You need plenty of rest for now, and I want to continue monitoring you."

"We'll see."

The doctor chuckled as though he didn't know what to make of that. "Yes, I suppose we will."

Ethan was happy to prove the guy wrong.

"How much time passed between when you were initially struck on the head and lost most of your memory and when you passed out?"

Ethan frowned. "A day, maybe a day and a half?"

He had been remembering things ever since. For the most part. It seemed to come in overwhelming rushes, but the nurse had said it was a good sign for his memory to return so quickly.

"And what were you doing during that day and a half?"

"Running. Hiking. Sleeping." Going through a dead man's clothing—more than one.

The doctor said, "How about we consider stress and overexertion may play a part in your being here? Now it's time to rest."

Ethan said, "Fair enough."

The doctor smiled.

He didn't like being told what to do or having anything about his life managed for him. It was why he'd gotten out of the Marines as soon as he could after that last disastrous mission. No one was willing to listen to the truth.

Serving from behind a desk was hardly the same as the job he had been doing before that mission. It would be like Nico suddenly becoming a house pet. A serious waste of her skills.

The doctor said, "There's a reason why, if you check yourself out, it's referred to as leaving 'against medical advice.'"

Ethan had nothing to say to that.

"I promise you won't be here any longer than necessary." The doctor said, "After that, it's up to you."

Ethan nodded.

"Let the nurse know if you need anything. Your pain medicine will wear off in a couple of hours, so you'll start feeling crummy pretty soon." He went to the door. "Try to get some rest. Who knows? More of your memory might return."

The door closed and all his energy seemed to drain out of him. Fine, so he wasn't okay.

Ethan lowered the bed to a forty-five degree angle and closed his eyes.

As if that would stop him from doing what he needed to do.

It was still easier to think without that visual input where the lights overhead pricked like pins in his eyes. He did not like being ill or injured. Brett was the same way. Like that time when they were eleven, and he'd fallen sideways off the ramp on his trick bike.

Brett had broken his wrist but refused to admit it. Ethan had told their mom, and Brett didn't speak to him for two days after she took him to the doctor. Just because his brother wanted to pretend everything was fine while Ethan felt the same pain, the way some twins did.

Was that some of what was happening now?

Maybe his brother was hurt somewhere. Like he'd hit his head and was confused. Maybe all of this pain—and the passing out—was because Brett lay somewhere hurt. It was either that or Ethan's issues were currently making his brother feel worse than he needed to.

Was Brett really lost in the woods?

Ethan didn't want to think the O'Callaghans might have found him. That wasn't a good thought, any more than the dream that seemed to slam into him. Memories trapped him in his sleep when he was supposed to be resting.

A knock on the door drew him to wakefulness. Then another, louder knock. The door handle twisted, and it eased open.

He tried to speak, but all that came out was a croak.

Kelly bit her lip. "That doesn't sound good."

"Water." He motioned to the table with his finger. "Please."

She held the straw to his lips, and he took a drink.

"I had a weird dream just now." He wanted to shake his head but didn't think that would be a good idea. "Maybe it wasn't a dream."

She leaned against the bed rail. "Want to tell me about it?"

He would rather hear about what happened with that marshal after he passed out. But if she was here and he wasn't cuffed to the bed, maybe everything had turned out okay.

Ethan said, "Brett was antsy. I could tell because it was making me feel the same way. He was pacing up and down the plane like he was trying to work something out."

"Did the plane crash by accident, or was it sabotage?"

He closed his eyes for a second. "I don't know, but it almost seemed like Brett wasn't surprised. After the crash, he was dragged off by that marshal from the car. Two others went after him. I was with the dead one." Ethan's thoughts drifted away, and his head started pounding.

"You don't need to worry about Edmonton," she said. "He's in police custody, where he can answer a whole lot of questions."

"How about whether or not my brother is even alive right now?"

She squeezed his arm. "Do you remember what happened after he was dragged off? How did you end up in the woods?"

"The other marshal, the dead one we found, he and I went after Brett. He told me that if I saw anyone I didn't like, I should run. Keep out of sight and stay safe." He frowned. "I don't even like saying it now any more than I liked hearing it then."

"So I'm guessing you're not the kind of person who sits around waiting for things to happen."

"The problem is that I have no idea who I can trust right now." He needed to be up, not lying in this hospital bed. "Did I see him get shot?"

Kelly said nothing.

Ethan sighed.

"You can trust me. And I mean that," she said. "I'm not just saying it because I want something."

Ethan said, "Does that mean we're going to look for Brett? Because I don't know that I trust anyone else to find him."

Kelly flinched. "We need to talk about that."

TEN

He stared at her, and she hesitated knowing he wouldn't like it. "I checked in with the marshals on my way over here. The ones I thought were already on their way." She'd sent everything she discovered to her boss, relaying it in an email. She'd also called her former captain from Chicago, but he hadn't phoned back. Yet.

"Okay." There was caution in his gaze.

"I was on the phone with the marshals from when Chief Filburn dropped me at my car all the way to pulling in the parking lot here. The flight details were kept under wraps, but I managed to locate the agent over the operation. He had no idea the plane had gone down here. No one was even looking for the aircraft."

Ethan's lips puffed out. "That's unbelievable."

"The whole transport was so secret there was a distinct lack of people at their office to notice that it went down." She shook her head. "He thought it wasn't leaving until tomorrow. No one put it together that the plane with their witness on it was the same one people had begun to report happened here, until I handed them that information."

It was either a high-security operation or designed because someone intended it to go unnoticed. At least at first. Thankfully the plane had crash-landed where people in her town saw it. Where first responders like her could move in and search. Find survivors, like Ethan, who had been fighting for his life with no idea why he was a target.

"Did you remember everything?"

He frowned. "A lot more. Not all of it, I don't think."

"The marshals are sending people. Everyone already here was on the plane, and the guy I spoke to said there were four agents. We know one is dead. There weren't any on that plane, just the dead pilot, and one of the agents is in custody. That means two are with Brett."

"The two I saw go after him," he said. "Hopefully they're protecting Brett from the others and all those guys O'Callaghan has running around the woods."

And the marshals with Brett hadn't called in at all, which Kelly figured meant they couldn't for one reason or another. Dead battery, like her before she'd charged her phone.

"Where's Nico?"

"I dropped her off in the police department kennel." Kelly smiled. The dog loved it there, because the officers all came by to say hi to her when they went in and out of the department. She'd had to instruct them on how to interact with her partner, but overall the cops liked having a K-9.

She had to convince the chief to get the mayor to sign off on the whole division.

Then her position here would be secure.

And yet, the fact her position in this department could've been created only because she'd been maneuvered so she was protected rubbed her the wrong way. Was she only here because her dad of all people had put in a call and pulled a favor from an old friend? Just so she would be hired and kept under the radar of the O'Callaghans without her knowing?

There had to be more to it than that, or she'd have been told they knew she was a cop so they were gunning for her. What more didn't she know?

Before she could get the conversation back on track, her phone rang. "Sorry."

Ethan waved his hand, and she answered her phone, taking a moment to look at him. He had more color than before. Maybe he was feeling much better. He seemed to be, but was he the guy who would even admit to her if he was feeling crummy?

"Officer Wayne."

His lips twitched. He thought the way she answered the phone was funny…or cute? Or was it how she'd studied him for a moment?

Kelly frowned as the caller said, "It's Captain Montgomery." Her former boss from Chicago had finally called her back.

"Yes, sir." She pushed off the bed rail and shoved off all the distraction Ethan amounted to, which was more than was okay for a police officer supposed to be protecting a witness. "Thank you for returning my call."

"Sounded serious."

She didn't waste time. "Can you tell me why I got shoved out of the O'Callaghan undercover operation two years ago, the real reason?"

He was quiet for a second, then said, "By the time it got to that point, the feds were involved. Brett had made a deal with them. It was out of my hands, but the going assumption was that he cut you out so he could take all the credit. Everyone figured he did you wrong so he could be the one to bring O'Callaghan down."

"He did cut me out." At least it was clear now that was precisely what'd happened. But so he could go into witness security and take all the credit? It didn't seem like a life of anonymity would achieve that unless he planned to go public at some point. Especially considering the fact they'd faked his death.

"Did anyone ever mention the O'Callaghans finding out I was a cop?"

"Not to my knowledge. Everyone was more concerned about the fact Brett suddenly died and keeping you safe as well. What's this about?"

"Sir, did my dad have any involvement at any point?"

"Not that I'm aware of."

Kelly frowned. "Anything else strange happen around that time?"

"Why do you ask, Officer Wayne?"

"Because it seems like a lot went on that I know nothing about, and I was purposely kept in the dark."

Her former captain was quiet again for a second.

"What is it?"

"I did have a meeting with one of the marshals shortly after Brett's 'death.' I'll have to see if I can remember the guy's name. He said he was going to your house to tell you in person what the result of all your hard work was."

She cringed. "That sounds ominous."

"At the time, I didn't think anything of it," he said. "I figured he wanted to thank you personally. You never said anything to me about it after, so I figured there was a nondisclosure agreement involved. You know how the feds are."

"I thought I did." She turned back and saw Ethan's attention on her, concern in his expression. "Can you remember anything about the guy?"

"Just that he seemed...gray."

Edmonton.

Was it really the same guy?

Kelly wrapped up the conversation and hung up. She stowed the phone. "You said you remember some, and I just need your gut reaction about Brett."

"Okay." He seemed to brace.

She didn't know why, since she had no idea what their dynamic was like. Twins should get along. Maybe they'd even be closer than a lot of other sibling-type relationships.

Kelly said, "Is Brett the kind of person to cut someone out and take all the credit for himself?"

Ethan frowned. "There has to be more to it than that."

She nodded. "Okay." His brother wouldn't be after simple glory. "We need to find him."

"I said that a short while ago. You clammed up." His brows lifted. "Care to tell me why that is?"

Kelly didn't want to. She blew out a breath. "I

can't take Nico, go out and find Brett. I've been ordered to stay away from the search."

He frowned. "Why?"

"The chief thinks I need to be protected. And I get taking backup, especially if you're with me. Going out if it's just us and Nico would be dangerous, considering the woods are crawling with O'Callaghan's guys. We don't even know if we can trust the marshals who are out there."

"But you still want to do it."

She wasn't going to lie. "Yes. I want to find your brother. More than I want to sit around waiting for someone else to."

After all the deception that got her to this place, she wanted to be honest with Ethan. He made her want to fight on his behalf. To employ every resource she had to help find his brother. To do the right thing so Brett could testify.

This had all started with the O'Callaghans. It would end with their operation being destroyed and Michael finally going to prison.

After that? Kelly didn't want to think about it. Ethan was enrolled in witness security. It wasn't like she would ever see him again.

Even if she wanted to.

At least she'd have the life she built here. Regardless of the fact it was based on deception, it was still the result of her hard work that she and Nico were a successful team. No one could take that away from her.

"So do I," Ethan said. "As soon as I'm let out of here."

She straightened. "We need to go see my dad."

Kelly pulled into the driveway of a square house with concrete front steps and a handrail. To Ethan it seemed like hours had passed since she'd told him this was what she wanted to do. It hadn't been that long, though it had taken him some time to get discharged from the hospital.

Over the front windows were shades that jutted out at an angle, what to him looked like thin strips of siding held up by iron brackets.

The front door had one of those doorbell cameras, so her dad would know they were there. Not out looking for Brett. *God, keep him safe.*

Nico bounced around in the back seat and barked once.

Kelly chuckled. "Let's go see Grandpa."

Ethan climbed out his door while she let the dog out of the rear compartment, using the little gate thing between the front seats. It was wide enough for the slender dog to step onto the center console and then jump out Kelly's door.

As he watched, Nico waited on the grass. Her body almost twitched with the need to run. Kelly stood for a second, saying nothing. The front door of the house opened. An older man stood there, the kind of guy Ethan would've thought to be a trucker—or a dockworker.

Kelly said, "Yes."

Nico raced for Kelly's father, but she didn't follow the dog.

Ethan wondered what she was thinking. The woman could be seriously frustrated that she wasn't allowed to go out and search for his brother for all he knew. About as much as he was, probably, though she didn't show it. Meanwhile he was about to explode like Nico had, released to go to Kelly's dad. And for what?

She looked at him, apparently in no hurry to go inside. "Sure you're okay enough to be out of the hospital?"

Ethan said, "I guess you've got the job of making sure I'm all right. And stay that way."

She rolled her eyes. "Great." Her lips curled up. "I also excel at accepting medical advice."

He found himself smiling. The doctor hadn't been happy that he'd left without spending the night, but they'd picked up the prescription of pain medication Ethan was given on the way here. That would keep the pounding in his head to a minimum. He hoped.

She studied him. "I should have trained Nico like one of those service dogs that can tell when there's a medical emergency."

He frowned. It was a nice idea, but for one glaring problem. "I think the dog has to be trained with the person, so they can spot the specific issue."

"I didn't say it was logical. Just *possible*."

"You must have driven Brett bonkers."

She twisted toward him. "What's that supposed to mean?"

He was worried down to his soul over his brother, even with the possibility that Brett had two US marshals currently protecting him. Still, something about Kelly made it seem as though everything in the world fell away, leaving only the two of them.

He shook his head. "It never would've worked between the two of you."

Kelly laughed, the nicest sound he'd heard in a long time. "Yeah, it was so not like that."

"No?"

"No way. Brett is a good cop, I guess. Working together was interesting, and I thought we got the job done because the operation ended, and he's testifying. Michael O'Callaghan is going to jail."

Why did it relieve him to know nothing had ever happened between her and his brother?

"You guys coming inside?" the trucker guy at the door called over.

"Yeah, Dad."

Ethan followed her to the door, considering his reaction. It was strange not to know why he was relieved, but maybe it didn't matter so much. Something in him knew it was good that she only seemed interested in him.

Not that it could go anywhere.

He didn't live here. He lived... Ethan had no idea. He didn't even know what he did for a living right now. Whatever occupation the US Marshals had cooked up for him.

They headed inside.

Kelly waved at her dad, then Ethan. "Bill Wayne, this is Ethan Harrigan."

"You look like your brother." The older man ambled down the hall as though the simple act of walking caused discomfort. It was hard to watch.

Kelly glanced at Ethan, who shut the front door behind him, and they followed the older man into a sparse kitchen. Bill got three mugs down. "Coffee?" He didn't turn, just poured their drinks.

"Sure." Ethan pulled out a chair from the kitchen table. He didn't want them to know how little energy he had, but Kelly didn't miss anything. "Black is good."

She waited until her dad handed them their mugs.

"What's up, baby girl?" Bill sat across from

Ethan while Kelly leaned her hips against the breakfast bar. Her mug was beside her on the counter, untouched.

"A federal witness is missing in the woods, and we don't know if he's dead or alive." Kelly leveled him with a stare. "But you know that, don't you? Because you know him."

"Don't worry about Brett." Bill took a sip. "He can take care of himself."

Ethan said, "You know the plane crashed?"

Bill looked at him and nodded.

"I am going to worry about my brother."

"That's because you're a better man than he is."

Ethan frowned. It was on the tip of his tongue to argue with the guy, but he had no idea what to say.

Kelly said, "Do you have any way to contact him or anyone on his detail? There are more marshals on their way here, but we need to make sure the witness gets to court on time. That means we have two days to find him, keep him safe and show up."

Bill shrugged. "Bit above my pay grade."

"You're retired." Kelly sighed. "Why did you tell Chief Filburn to keep me safe? You moved here first. Did you manipulate me here as well?"

"The chief and I—"

"I know you're old friends," she said.

A dog door flap pushed up, and Nico trotted inside. She went to Bill and sat with her back to his leg. The older man ran a hand down the dog's head.

"Why didn't you tell me I was in danger?" Kelly said. "Nico and I could find Brett, but we're locked down from searching because the chief told me the O'Callaghans found out I was a cop." The dog's ears perked up, probably at hearing her name coupled with that command. "So I'm being sidelined, and Ethan is left to worry if his brother is even alive."

Ethan didn't like the idea of Brett being hurt or dead. He should be protecting his twin. Everything in him was drawn in that direction, like a radar beacon. Probably the whole reason he'd been with Brett.

Their identical faces made Ethan as much of a target as Brett. He would've had no choice but to go into witness security.

"You knew they made me," she said. "They knew I was a cop."

Bill nodded.

"So why not just tell me? It makes no sense to keep me in the dark."

"No?" Bill shot her a pointed look Ethan didn't get.

"Why was keeping the truth from Kelly the better idea?" Ethan figured she needed to know, as much as he did. Maybe more. Right now his brain cried out for information while she wanted *answers*. There was a difference.

"They would've killed you. And you would've done your job no matter what." Bill sniffed. "I wasn't going to lose you as well."

Kelly's eyes shimmered with tears.

"The O'Callaghans weren't going to rest until they got their—"

Nico set off toward the hall, barking.

Kelly pushed off the counter and headed after her K-9. "Someone is here."

Ethan didn't want her going alone. He started to rise from the chair when she called back from the hall.

"Get down!"

Gunfire erupted at the front of the house— a steady stream of automatic rifle fire. Ethan hit the deck before realizing he'd gotten on the floor. He covered his head with his hands and listened to the shooting.

"Kelly!"

She didn't answer.

ELEVEN

Kelly covered Nico's head with her hands. Her entire body clenched as the front of the house exploded. Shot after shot sent glass and drywall across her.

Someone outside shouted. The shots stopped.

She started to get up, but the door flew open. It slammed against the wall and dark figures raced in.

She turned enough to see a gun pointed directly at her face. Kelly reached for the weapon on her hip. It wasn't there and neither was her police shield because she wasn't on duty. Something that might save her life depending on what this was—and if they knew she was a cop. Some criminals would kill a person when they discovered they were a cop.

The only way to fight back was the gun in the car, given she'd assumed her dad's house to be a safe place.

Won't happen again.

Nico shifted from under her, got up on all fours and shook the debris from her fur. She leaned forward and growled at the intruder.

Dark eyes narrowed and a low voice said, "That dog comes at me, and it gets shot."

There were a number of things Kelly wanted to say. She held them all back and kept her mouth shut. Ethan and her father were in the kitchen. She needed to make sure they were all right.

She saw a flash of his teeth on a stern face. One she recognized. "Don't test me."

This was Franko O'Callaghan, the patriarch's first cousin. Michael had taken over from his father, but Franko had been their enforcer since Michael was a baby.

Kelly said, "Nico, leave it."

The dog backed down, barely a fraction. Kelly got up and put her hand on the dog's head. She was the alpha, and that meant she was the one who protected the pack. As soon as Nico felt that from her, she relaxed. Just not enough she sat. The dog wouldn't drop her guard.

Not the way she'd done with Ethan.

If Kelly needed a way to tell if he was trustworthy, Nico's opinion was it.

Franko motioned with his gun. "Where's the brother?"

Kelly went first into the kitchen, Nico moving with her as though Kelly held an invisible lead. "Ethan, you okay?"

He shifted and got to his feet, brushing off his hair. He did look a little pale.

When he saw the men enter the kitchen behind her, he backed up a step. "What is this about?"

"What do you think?" Franko said.

Kelly didn't see her father, and the back door was slightly ajar. Did he go out in the back to hide? She couldn't believe he'd have run off.

Just before the gunshots had erupted, he'd been about to say something. The O'Callaghans had wanted...what?

She had nothing they'd want. Thanks to Brett she wasn't the one testifying.

What could they possibly be after except maybe the money mentioned a couple of times? She didn't know anything about it. Ethan might, but he'd have to remember first.

She was at a loss as to why these guys were here instead of in the woods looking for Brett.

"This is my dad's house. We have no idea why you're here, Franko." His name slipped from her mouth.

Franko whipped around. "That's right. It is you." His expression shifted. "That's what the call was about."

But he hadn't come here looking for her?

"Congratulations, you found me." Let him think she had no idea what was going on. It wasn't untrue, but she doubted that was why he'd shown up here. "Now what do you want?"

"We're going for a ride."

Kelly's whole being rejected that idea.

He leveled the gun at her. Ethan shifted, like he wanted to intervene.

Kelly lifted her hand, hoping that was enough. "It's okay." She could figure out a way to resolve this. "But you need to tell us what's going on."

"You think I *need* to tell you anything?" Franko scoffed. "Move." He motioned with the gun. "And bring the dog."

"Why—"

Franco grabbed her arm and shoved the gun at the underside of her chin.

"Okay." She lifted her hands. "If you walk me out like this, Nico isn't going to let you get far. You have to let me walk with her."

It sounded good. She wasn't sure how true it was, but being free of his grasp gave her more of a chance to figure out how they would get out of this situation.

She said, "If you tell me what you want then I can be prepared."

He frowned at her. "I said you'd be more trouble than you're worth, *Sara*."

Yeah, that was her undercover name.

"And I didn't even know then that you were a cop." He sneered.

She wanted to ask who told them, or how they'd found out. Maybe she didn't want to know. Then again, there was so much going on here that she might have to save the questions until later.

"Where is my brother?" Ethan's question brought her attention to him. Nico stood beside him, guarding him. The way she'd told Nico to do in the car. It seemed as though the dog still considered him to be someone worth protecting.

I agree.

Franko said, "That's what the dog will tell us." He shoved her. "Now go."

"Nico." Kelly clicked her fingers.

The dog didn't move.

"Ethan, you need to go first. We'll follow."

Under armed guard, they walked down her dad's hallway to the front door. Part of her wondered if her dad got away and managed to call the cops. Would there be a swarm of officers outside, waiting to pick up Franko and these men?

She didn't want to be in a hostage situation. It couldn't be helped unless she got herself and Ethan—and Nico—out of this.

"Bring whatever you need to search for Brett. Because your dog is the one that's going to find him."

At the front door she glanced back at Franko. "Who told you that?"

"Does it matter? I know the mutt can do it."

He shoved at her and she stumbled out the front door into Ethan. He caught her, but she had to pull away so these guys didn't think he could be used as leverage against her—as well as his brother.

They had to believe he was just another innocent bystander as far as she was concerned.

Kelly practically pushed him away. He frowned, but once she explained it would make sense.

"If Nico is going to find Brett, I need a few things." She wanted to fold her arms or put her hands on her hips, but she was in no position to make demands here. "Supplies. Something that belongs to Brett that Nico can scent. We'll have to go to the crash site. After we go to my house."

Franko lifted his chin in the direction of her car. "Open the trunk."

Before she could argue, one of his guys reached in by the steering wheel and popped the rear door. Did they know about the socks Ethan had found her on the plane? Those were in her backpack, passenger side, up front on the floor.

He lifted out a duffel from inside Nico's compartment that was her bag of supplies for working with Nico. He tossed it at her and she caught it.

He didn't know about the socks.

Kelly said, "I still need a scent from Brett. Otherwise Nico doesn't know what to find."

The dog shifted against Ethan's side. He laid a hand on her head, frowning at Kelly. She couldn't explain what she was doing, which left both of them frustrated.

O'Callaghan said, "You expect me to believe you don't already have one?"

She spun around to Franko and met his fist.

Pain exploded on the left side of her face. Kelly blinked at the ground and realized she'd fallen to her hands and knees.

Nico sniffed her ear.

"I'm okay." Kelly managed to get the words out. *Ouch*. That hurt a lot.

"Good," Franko said. "Let's go. And you wanna play me again? Now we know what happens."

She got to her feet and swayed.

Ethan's eyes were like fire.

"Done messing me around, *Officer*?"

She kept her mouth closed.

"Good. Let's go."

Kelly grabbed the duffel from the guy and strode to the vehicle at the curb. "Fine."

The SUV raced down streets through town, back toward the highway according to signs

Ethan saw on the side of the road and turns they took. He wanted to be sick. Kelly's face had swollen on one side, her cheek all red.

He couldn't reach over and comfort her. And he'd figured out why she pulled away from him.

They couldn't afford for the O'Callaghans to believe Ethan and Kelly meant something to each other.

Aside from the fact they barely knew one another, and there wasn't anything between them, it could easily look like they cared.

A relationship wasn't in the cards for him. Not after that whole Alice debacle.

"What was that?"

Ethan glanced over. "What?"

Kelly frowned. "You just said Alice."

"I did?" He became aware everyone in the vehicle was listening. Meanwhile he found he could actually remember a few things about his past. He recalled being in uniform and Alice standing in front of him wearing a white dress.

"I met her a long time ago." He shook his head. "We used to be married."

These guys didn't need to know it ended about as fast as it'd begun. Alice hadn't been interested in standing beside him through the bad. Just the good.

Kelly shifted in her seat. She moved her attention to the road in front of them, and he realized he hadn't said anything about how his marriage ended. So long ago now he hardly remembered.

Nico sat between the middle row captain's chairs. The dog hadn't let her focus lapse, and it reminded Ethan to stay on his game. He couldn't let anything—least of all the beautiful, injured woman beside him—make him lose focus.

Seeing her go down like that had rocked him. Still, it was better than any of them getting shot. He prayed her dad had his phone on him and that the police were even now speeding after them. Her dad's house was toast, the entire front nothing but bullet holes. It was a wonder they hadn't been killed.

The sound had been all too familiar, like the rush of adrenaline that spelled danger. He knew how to handle himself but felt like he had a job to do and no tools to do it with. No weapons to fight the battle. And the holes in his memory weren't helping.

Alice was his wife. They'd divorced.

Ethan tried to remember.

Years ago, he thought. Long enough she barely registered now. Then again, it was all Kelly and nothing else. Not even Brett and the fact his brother could be in danger factored when a woman had been punched in the face by the guy now in the front seat. The one who'd turned to her and was glaring.

Ethan wanted to put a fist in *his* face. What had she called him? Franko O'Callaghan. He was one of them, then. Those people trying to kill his brother in order to keep him from testifying.

And yet, it seemed like there was more to it.

Something everyone wanted to know. Like where that money was they'd heard mentioned. Was that what Kelly's dad had been about to say before the shooting started?

Ethan needed them to talk. He figured he'd get the conversation started. "We're going to the crash site, right? So we can get something of Brett's." He did want to find his brother. "I can identify what's his. Nico can get a scent off anything, right?"

Kelly kept her gaze forward. "Certain things carry a scent better than others. Even if you hold a pen in your hand every day, she'll still get a better scent from the shirt you wear to bed."

Franko leveled his gun at Kelly. "Which turn to the crash site?"

She pressed her lips into a thin line and looked out the windows. "Two exits up. Take a right."

"Got it." The driver spoke for the first time.

They followed her directions to the gravel lane that led into the woods. When she told them to park because the rest of the journey was on foot, Franko said, "How far?"

"A mile or two. I don't know. I wasn't counting. I was helping Ethan get to the vehicle."

And she'd been dealing with that US marshal, Edmonton, the one the chief had arrested. Ethan couldn't remember the other two marshals—the ones still out there. He couldn't even recall their faces.

After they parked, she clipped a leash on Nico.

They walked to the airplane as a group, finding it much the same as they had before, void of people—cops or more of O'Callaghan's guys. He remembered that tattooed guy shooting his friend, and then Ethan had shoved him down the river. He shivered at the images in his head.

His prescription bottle was in Kelly's car.

Ethan figured this wasn't going to be fun at all. Pretty soon his head would explode, and they would probably kill him for being deadweight.

He meant nothing to these people. They only wanted Brett and *the money*.

The words came to him in a flash. Nothing else, just the idea there was cash involved in this. It wasn't just about his brother testifying. This was about O'Callaghan getting his money back.

Ethan glanced at Kelly, but she didn't see.

He needed to tell her. Only they were at

the plane, and Franko grabbed his arm. Ethan wanted to know where the police department was. Not to mention why the marshals hadn't even known the plane went down.

This whole situation was a disaster. Except he had met Kelly. That wasn't something he'd complain about, though he'd have lived without the memory loss and the concussion.

"You have two minutes. Get something the dog can use to find your brother."

Ethan got a weird sense of déjà vu. The last time they were in the plane he'd shot at a guy out the door and saved Kelly.

Ethan held on to the seat backs while he moved down the plane. He needed to stall so the local cops, who surely knew Kelly was out here in trouble, could show up. "You think Brett knows where O'Callaghan's money is."

"You could've taken it for yourself. Did you think of that?"

Franko apparently didn't have much consideration for sibling relationships. "You think I'd do that to my brother—my twin?"

"Like there's any love lost between you."

"We're working on it." Ethan frowned. It was as though he knew everything about himself, but it had a lid on it. Things came out by rote, but he couldn't pry the seal to dig for himself. It had to surface on its own.

He blew out a breath over the frustration of it all.

"You'd rather do that than take two mill?"

Ethan bit the inside of his lip. *Two million dollars?* "You think Brett has it? I'd know if he did. And trust me, the guy isn't sitting on a pile of cash. The marshals would've seen it in his suitcase. Don't you think?"

Franko was about to explode when someone from outside yelled, "Cops!"

He raced to the window to look outside.

Ethan ran for the back of the plane, where he remembered there being a hatch. *Yes.* He hauled the handle around, shoved it open and then ducked back into the lavatory. He eased the door open enough that an inch of light entered the tiny bathroom, but it was impossible to know what was happening outside.

A shadow crossed the floor.

Then a gun. "Come out, or I shoot you where you stand."

Just another step.

As soon as Franko stood in the right spot, Ethan flung the door open and launched himself at the guy.

The gun went off.

TWELVE

Muzzle flash flared in the windows inside the airplane.

"Keep your hands up!"

Kelly faced down the two police officers currently arresting Franko's friends.

"Wayne!" Chief Filburn looked like he didn't know whether to be mad at her or glad she was alive.

One of the officers glanced down at her dog, then lowered his gun. The other had one of Franko's men on the ground, and another of the shooters had run off. She'd been about to chase him when they stopped her.

She waved to the airplane, her hands still mostly in the air. "I need to check on Ethan. He's inside with an O'Callaghan."

Where a gun had already gone off.

Fear rippled through her like a living thing the way wind blew through the trees and left a chill behind in the mountain air.

Was he dead?

Chief Filburn said, "Let's go, Wayne."

"Nico." The dog jumped to her feet. Kelly grabbed the lead and walked the dog to the door with her boss in front. He had a gun, so he went first.

Given the look he shot her before he stepped inside, she knew she'd have to explain everything later. Namely why she was back out here instead of watching over Ethan at the hospital. Safe. Protected.

"Come on." She said it more to herself than to the K-9, and they moved inside the airplane.

The chief headed down the aisle, gun out, to the open door at the back, by the bathroom.

"Two exits?" She hadn't noticed when she'd been in the plane the last time.

"On an aircraft this size?" The chief shrugged. "It's not unusual."

Kelly said, "So they went outside?"

He stepped over the bulkhead door. She did the same and hopped down onto the grass. Both of them looked around. He said, "Who is out here?"

"Ethan and O'Callaghan's goons. He grabbed us at my dad's house."

Chief Filburn grimaced. "Why did they bring you out here?"

"To find something to track Brett, but I was

just stalling hoping you'd realize and catch up."
She frowned. "Did my dad call you?"

He shook his head. "I haven't heard from him.
We came back out to check out the wreckage
and we found you."

"The O'Callaghans are looking for something. Not just Brett. This is about more than
keeping him from testifying."

Filburn nodded. "They think Brett stole two
million dollars from them."

She whirled around. "If they found out I was
a cop, why don't they think I stole it?"

No one had been gunning for her since the
cave. Instead it seemed as if they only wanted
to use Nico to find Brett. They knew who she
was, but it was only an interesting piece of information to Franko. No one had asked her anything about the money.

Which meant they thought the witness knew
where it was. If they couldn't find Brett, she
didn't factor? Maybe.

"It was after you were out. Brett cut you loose
and then it seemed like everything that could've
gone wrong did." The chief shrugged one shoulder.

"How do you know this?"

"The marshals called and filled me in." Filburn said, "O'Callaghan was bleeding money,
and a chunk of it went missing. A big chunk.

Everyone points fingers at everyone else in an organization like that. You were gone, so no one was looking at you. But O'Callaghan thinks Brett knows where it is because he hasn't been able to find it. And he might want revenge on you for being a cop, but the money comes first. Money always comes first."

Kelly blew out a long breath. "Ethan is caught in the middle of all of this."

One of the officers called out from inside the plane.

She turned to the chief. "I need to find him. Get him back and keep him safe."

"This whole thing could be about dragging you in and using you, because they don't care what's left when they're done."

She lifted her chin. "I don't want Ethan to get hurt. I'm not being cut out again. I'm a good cop, and I have to do this."

"Let's go, then." Filburn glanced back. "Secure the area and take these guys in."

The officer nodded.

Filburn started walking.

She hurried alongside him into the trees. "If we're quick, we can catch up. I don't like leaving Ethan with Franko O'Callaghan any longer than necessary."

The chief stumbled. "Franko is here?"

She frowned as they strode quickly out of

sight of the plane. She didn't want to ditch their hope of backup any more than he did, but he was right. They needed someone to take suspects into custody. The chief and her might not see eye to eye all the time, but he'd been a solid boss.

Apparently he'd been protecting her for years, so she would continue to trust him.

After all, innocent lives were on the line.

Nico picked up on something and moved ahead of her. Kelly and the chief both broke into a jog. "What's the deal with Franko?"

"He's just bad news, that's all."

She didn't want to believe her dad had lied to her, or even withheld something—more than what she'd already learned. But the truth was it looked like that was exactly what'd happened. "Will Franko kill Ethan when he doesn't need him anymore?"

"Absolutely."

Kelly picked up her pace. They could get Brett to the courthouse themselves, make sure O'Callaghan and all his guys were taken down. But that meant Brett had to be alive to testify.

Despite that drive to find justice, Kelly noticed a shift in her. She needed to find Ethan more than she needed justice. After all this time spent wanting them brought down, needing to see the case finally finished and their organization taken apart, all she could think about was Ethan.

Only because he was an innocent caught up in this. Not because she wanted him to stick around after it was all done or anything. Even if she wanted to get to know him better that didn't mean it would ever happen.

Like getting Brett to the courthouse, she stared down the barrel of insurmountable odds.

But she wouldn't quit. Her dad had raised her to see every challenge, count the cost and then take each step needed to climb that mountain all the way to the top. *Give me the strength, Lord.* For Ethan's sake, and for justice, she could trust God for strength and wisdom.

She spotted Ethan ambling up ahead on the trail, hands out to his sides. Behind him, Franko had a gun pointed at his back. They were making sluggish progress. *Thank You, Lord.* It didn't take much time to catch up to them.

"Franko O'Callaghan!"

The guy whirled around at her call.

"Drop the gun!" the chief yelled.

When Franko moved his aim to her and fired, the chief squeezed off a shot. It rang through the air as she dived to the ground.

The chief ran to Franko.

Kelly scrambled up and headed for Ethan. The chief kicked Franko's gun away. She grabbed it for safekeeping—and because she didn't like not being armed.

Nico rushed Ethan. He put both hands out and the dog jumped, landing her front paws in his palms. He grinned. "Hey, girl, did you find me?"

The squeeze around Kelly's heart eased a fraction. "She did. Now it's time for her to find Brett."

His expression darkened. Nico jumped down and sat beside his leg.

Kelly motioned to the deer trail up ahead. "If you're up for a walk through the woods."

"If you are, then I am. And I want to find my brother."

Kelly nodded. "Chief?"

He straightened. Franko lay on the ground, dead. She felt her brows rise. "I thought you just winged him."

"He was gonna kill you. I did what I had to do." He lifted his chin. "Now let's find that witness."

Ethan was all in to find Brett. When Kelly glanced at him, he nodded. Tried to get a handle on the adrenaline now coursing through him. He laid his hand on Nico's head, finding solace in the dog's presence.

"Nico, come."

He moved with the dog, and Kelly said, "You okay?" She shifted the leash in her hands. "Did he hurt you?"

Ethan didn't want to be helpless. "I'm not much more injured than I was earlier."

"But you should still be lying down, resting. Right?"

Of course she was going to pull that card. "It would take too long to go back, and you need to be out here finding Brett." Preferably before O'Callaghan's men did to Ethan's brother what Kelly's chief had done.

Franko O'Callaghan had been about to kill the chief or Kelly. It would be written up in the police report as a "good shoot" or however they labeled it that meant it was justified—because it had been. And considering what the guy had threatened to do to Ethan, he didn't mind so much that the guy was dead. Apparently Franko had skill with knives.

Ethan was glad he didn't have to defend himself, unarmed, against a blade.

"He's right," the chief said. "Let's put that dog to work."

Kelly held his gaze for a second, then commanded Nico to find Brett using the item he gave her from the plane—a shirt that had belonged to his brother.

The dog jumped into action, sniffing the ground around them.

Ethan just prayed Brett had walked this way. It had been more than a day since the plane crash, past time for his twin and the marshals with him to get to safety and call in. So where was he?

Usually, Ethan was out of contact, being deployed several times during his stint of service. Brett had asked him to stay a few days every time he came home. Ethan quickly realized it was the best thing. They both felt the equilibrium of being together, and how it settled the restlessness inside them after a couple of days in each other's company. Usually they went camping.

They'd need another one of those trips after all this—something the marshals hadn't let them do since they enrolled together in witness security. No way had either of them considered never seeing each other again. He couldn't imagine not having his brother in his life, so even though it upended everything to find out Brett's life was in danger, Ethan went with him.

The rush of memory felt like walking into a sticky spider web.

Pride that his brother was doing the right thing. Worry over why Brett decided now to do something good like testifying—and protect himself in the process. Not to mention what

Brett hadn't told him because there was always something Brett held back. The guy was more complicated than anyone Ethan had ever met.

The chief moved to walk alongside him. "Do you mind answering a few questions?"

Ethan shrugged. "Talking it through might be a good idea."

If he didn't get a distraction, he would wind up wallowing in what he'd be left with if Brett was no longer alive. That wasn't something Ethan would ever be okay with. The loss of a family member wasn't easy for anyone. He didn't want to consider his situation so much worse because they were twins, but it was a special bond.

Where are you, Brett?

He had no idea if he'd feel it if his brother was dead. Ethan didn't want to find out.

The chief kept pace with him. "What can you tell me about Brett's state of mind before the plane went down?"

Both of them watched around them, looking for O'Callaghan's guys. Kelly strode in front, moving fast with Nico. Ethan wanted to watch her back, but with no weapon all he could do was warn her if someone was coming.

It didn't sit right not to be the one protecting others. Usually it was the other way around. As a history teacher he protected the high schoolers in his charge in a way, influencing how they saw the world and the past.

Ethan blew out a long breath.

"What is it?" The chief asked the question, but up ahead Kelly glanced back.

He looked at her when he said, "I became a history teacher in WITSEC. I was getting my credentials after I left the Marines, and they helped fast-track it."

"You remembered."

She had a great smile.

The chief said, "And your brother?"

Ethan had no idea what Brett did these days. Nothing related to law enforcement certainly. "What other questions did you have?"

"How did Brett seem?"

"Not more anxious than I'd have expected for someone putting their life on the line to testify."

The chief glanced over. "And the marshals with you guys on the plane? Were any of them acting off?"

"We already know at least one was dirty, right? The one you arrested."

Something flashed in the chief's eyes. "Right. I was just wondering about the others. Not the ones who just showed up, but those on the plane."

Ethan tried to think. The pounding in his head was so incessant it became like a consistent beat that he could eventually ignore if he tried hard enough not to think about it. But that only left him with the rest of his body. He was past exhausted and sick to his stomach.

If they did go camping, he would likely sleep the whole time. But considering his brother would be watching his back, it would be some of the best sleep he'd had in a long time. Although, given how much time he'd spent in the woods the last few days something else might be better.

"There's someone up ahead," Kelly called back.

When they caught up to her, she said, "Ethan can you stay with Nico? The chief and I will make sure it's clear."

They moved ahead, and he held Nico's leash. Ethan didn't stay where he was. He just hung back, sticking with Nico.

"Got a body," the chief called back.

His heart clenched.

"It's one of the marshals. He's unconscious, but alive."

"I found Brett!" Kelly picked up her pace.

They heard a roar, and the chief said, "Police!"

Ethan took cover behind a tree, then saw a man drop a gun. "I'm a marshal."

He came out from behind the cover and brought Nico to Kelly. "Where is—"

"There." Kelly pointed.

Ethan saw his brother, lying face down on the ground. He raced over and turned Brett to his back. The cry left his lips without him acknowledging it. Tears gathered, blurring his brother's battered face. "What did they do to you?"

He held Brett's cheeks and lowered his head to touch their foreheads.

The inhale came from deep in Brett's chest. He launched up, shoving Ethan back. Brett cried out and grabbed Ethan.

"Whoa. I've got you." He held tight to his brother, everything in him never wanting to let go of the one person in the world who understood what it was like to be him. Through the good and the bad, they were brothers.

Brett gripped him right back, breathing hard.

A second later his eyes rolled back in his head, and he passed out.

THIRTEEN

Kelly strode into the emergency department, looking for Ethan. She should be more worried about the federal witness and the case against Michael O'Callaghan, but the truth was that Ethan remained at the forefront of her mind.

It had taken longer to get here because she'd had the chief drop her off at the PD to kennel Nico and had to get her own car from her dad's house. Having her police shield on her belt and her gun on her hip—whether she could use it effectively or not—made her feel better. More like herself. Nico was okay resting.

She kept repeating that in her mind, but in reality, it was Kelly who wasn't okay. She preferred having her partner with her.

Something about Nico kept her steady in a way a human cop partner never had.

A romantic relationship could be like that—a source of strength. The kind of gift God could give her.

And why did that make her think of Ethan?

It was getting harder and harder to contemplate the fact she'd have to say goodbye to him soon enough. He would go back to his life. She'd have to figure out the mess that was hers. Probably she'd remember him for the rest of her life, always wondering what could've been.

It was a sad but comforting sentiment.

And one that meant she didn't notice when the chief came up beside her with that frown on his face she realized meant he worried about her. Before he could ask if she was okay—a question she didn't want to answer—Kelly said, "How are Brett and the marshal?"

She looked around for Ethan but didn't see him.

"Getting checked out," the chief said. "The brother is with Brett."

"Good." She'd tried calling her dad a couple of times, but his phone had been off or out of battery. Something about her boss and his actions the last few hours held her tongue instead of her asking him if he'd seen her father.

Kelly felt the need to keep things to herself until she knew more. This whole situation seemed like everyone was far more interested in the money than keeping the patriarch's first-born son, Michael, out of prison.

Maybe they were all trying to get it for themselves.

"What do we know about the state of O'Callaghan's operation right now?"

The chief frowned. "We'd need to ask the marshals or Chicago PD."

"I should call my old captain again. Find out if there's infighting. That would explain why there are so many guys here." She shook her head. "And if we knew which marshals we could trust it would help us keep Brett safe."

"I'm more interested in keeping you safe and out of it."

"Because my dad told you to look out for me?"

"I didn't give you a job because of pity." He folded his arms. "You're a good cop. But back when your dad and I were working together, it was a different world. A grayer one."

She wasn't sure she agreed with that. "Justice is justice."

"Depends who is dishing it out as to what that looks like."

She nodded. "Okay, that's true. But we can't let O'Callaghan run the show."

His expression darkened. "I know what happens when he's allowed free rein."

"So why wouldn't you be all in to take him down?"

"You can't fight a guy like that. He has reach. Until he's dead we'll all be watching our backs every day of our lives. That's why you're not going anywhere near this trial or the business of missing money."

Kelly frowned. "We need officers to keep Brett Harrigan and his brother safe. We can't allow him to miss that court hearing. If we can't trust all the marshals, then we can't trust any of them. So we make sure that it happens. We have to get him to court."

"Not our problem."

"Because you're scared of Michael O'Callaghan."

The chief leaned in, a blank expression on his face, probably to hide the depth of the truth from her. "Yes. I am."

She was about to ask him what had happened to make him so fearful of the guy when her phone rang. The screen said, *Dad*.

When Kelly lifted her head to tell the chief, he was gone. She said, "Dad?"

"Did anyone hear you say that?" His voice sounded breathy like he was moving.

Kelly frowned and turned around. "No. What's going on?"

"I'm sorry, okay? About everything." He sighed, blowing across the microphone. "I have to go, and you might not see me for a while."

"You're running."

"O'Callaghan will figure out I'm here. That puts more than just you in danger." He let out a frustrated sound. "Everything went wrong when that plane came down. You should've stayed away and not gone out searching."

"As if I'd sit at home and fail to do my job." She couldn't believe he'd think she would do that. He'd practically trained her to be a cop with all the self-defense and trips to the range to learn how to handle guns safely. And he was surprised when she wanted to do her job?

It made no sense.

"You need to tell me what's going on, Dad. I'm flying blind here."

"I'm sorry, honey." He cleared his throat. "I didn't do the right thing before. I was scared and I just wanted to protect you."

"Did you take the two million from O'Callaghan?" She couldn't believe her father, a retired cop and the best man she knew, would have. But right now it felt like she didn't know anything.

Was this how Ethan felt when he didn't even know who he was?

"If I could tell you," he said, "I would. But it's safer if you don't know."

"You can't possibly think that's true." She shook her head and paced the hallway.

"Stay safe, honey. Keep your eyes open." He took a breath. "Stay away from any O'Callaghans."

The line went dead.

Kelly turned around in the hallway, but her chief was still nowhere to be seen. Where had he gone? She was alone in the hall. The way she'd felt when Brett cut her out of the undercover investigation.

Kelly strode to the nurse's desk and flashed her badge. She asked for his room number and was pointed in the right direction. She half expected the room to be empty, but Brett lay in the bed. Ethan sat in a chair beside it, concern on his face.

They'd been talking.

"I'm interrupting." But she was so glad to see them. Everything in her was drawn to Ethan. It was like she needed to be where he was.

It would be so easy to lean on him because she was in a crisis right now and felt like she had nothing to anchor herself to. But that wasn't fair to either of them. And how would it help when she had to let him go?

Ethan gave her a soft smile. "It's okay. Come in, because you probably want to hear this."

Brett was pretty beat-up, which she figured was from a run-in with O'Callaghan's men. But from the curious look he gave Ethan and then her, he'd picked up on whatever Kelly was currently trying to deny.

"I do need a statement." It was better she kept this about work.

That might be the only way her heart was going to survive.

Ethan spotted the shift in her. He didn't know if it was for Brett's benefit. Maybe the professional version of Kelly, the one who was a cop only, would put his brother at ease.

He'd rather have stuck with the woman underneath, who was a cop through and through. Flaws, weaknesses and all. The one who showed her strength when she was at that weakest moment.

He much preferred her.

Brett frowned at him. Ethan gave him a tiny shake of his head. His twin had been dragged into the woods and hurt. He had a job to do. Ethan was only with him because he'd be in more danger elsewhere and the marshals hadn't had enough assigned agents to split their focus like that.

Kelly moved to the end of Brett's bed. "It's been a minute."

Brett made a noise in his throat. "It sure has."

"You know I hated you for most of the last two years, right? Once I figured out that you weren't dead, but the one who was going to testify, I realized I had to figure out how to forgive you. I'm working on it."

Brett smiled slightly. "It was the right thing to do after they found out who you were. We didn't need to all be caught up in this. Now it's ruined mine and Ethan's lives."

Ethan frowned. "I never said that."

"So you were happy about giving up everything including your shot at getting Alice back and going into hiding with me?"

"That was two years ago. And it was over with Alice long before that." Why had Brett even brought her up?

Oh.

He thought Kelly would be another Alice? Ethan studied the woman. She didn't seem happy their conversation had drifted to talking about a woman, even if it was someone who meant nothing to Ethan other than that she'd played a role in his past. Alice had taught him what he *didn't* want in a woman.

And if Brett thought Kelly was anything like his bygone days' ex-wife, he didn't know her at all, even though they'd worked together.

Ethan kind of liked that. It meant he knew her better than his twin did.

"We have a lot to talk about," Kelly said. "So

we'll start with the money everyone is looking for. Who took it?"

Brett blew out a breath. "The less you know about that, the safer everyone will be." But instead of indicating everyone, he motioned toward Ethan.

"That's the immediate issue," Kelly said. "The rest is just paperwork after the fact. So tell me if I need to worry about more of O'Callaghan's guys coming after the both of you for that two million, or did you tell them where to find it?"

Brett's eyes flashed.

Ethan said, "He didn't tell them, but he doesn't like what he did say."

His brother's head whipped around. Brett touched his nose. "You're not supposed to translate."

"I'm not letting you keep things quiet that need to be out. We can trust Kelly." He should've said Officer Wayne, just to keep things professional like they probably should be, but it was too late now.

Brett said, "I know that. It's why I think you should stay with her, and I'll go with the marshals and give my testimony in court."

Ethan stared at his brother.

"You guys can protect each other while I do what I need to."

Kelly said, "How do you even know you can trust the marshals? Two of them did this to you."

"Only one was dirty, and the other shot him."

"That seems to be a theme with these guys." Kelly nodded. "Okay. So what's the rest of it?"

"Like I said, the more you know, the more danger you're in."

She shook her head. "Is that why you shut me out two years ago? Cut me from the case and nearly ruined my whole career?"

Ethan grimaced. Brett said, "Your dad was my training officer."

"So you knew him." Kelly's expression blanked. "But the O'Callaghans found out I was a cop?"

Brett nodded. "Not just that, but the O'Callaghans killed your mother."

Kelly frowned. "She was stabbed in a mugging."

She had stiffened. Ethan studied her, silently praying. This couldn't be anything good.

"That's what your dad told you, right?" Brett said. "But Thomas O'Callaghan, Michael's father, had her killed because your dad was putting the pressure on. Trying to get a conviction. And he was close, because Thomas ordered the hit on your mom."

"If that's true I'd never have been selected for that undercover op." Kelly lifted her hands.

Ethan figured she had a point about that. It would've been in her police file, right?

Brett said, "Your dad didn't find out until you were deep in. He called me as soon as he did, but I already thought he knew. We made a deal to get you out."

"Without telling her," Ethan said.

Kelly sniffed. "I'm sick to death of people keeping things from me." Tears gathered in her eyes. "If they killed my mother, they'd have known who I was the minute I walked in."

Brett shook his head. "Thomas was dead by then. Michael didn't care about the old ways or ancient vendettas. I always thought your dad did it. But when I asked, he denied it."

Kelly shook her head. "You're unbelievable."

"It's the truth," Brett continued. "His son was in charge then. Michael doesn't care about the past. He only cares about women and making money. That was why we had to take him down. That drug of his was killing people, and it hit the women he sold first. He didn't even care."

Kelly said nothing. Ethan wanted to go to her, pull her into his arms. He stayed in his seat so Brett could finish telling the story.

"When your dad found out what we were doing, he called me. Convinced me to get you out," Brett said. "We were close enough that I had what I needed to end it."

"And the money?"

He shook his head. "I can't talk about that. I just have to testify, and then everything will be fine. Michael will be behind bars where he belongs."

"But that doesn't mean a guy like him couldn't come after you." Ethan had heard the marshals talking about the kind of reach he had.

"They're falling apart," Brett said. "Everyone wants the money, so the family is collapsing. Everyone is murdering the person in their way and searching for the money themselves so they can keep it."

"No one cares about keeping him out of prison?" Kelly asked.

"All this, the crash and everything, is about the money." Brett let out a sigh, as though exhausted from the talking. "That's why I have to keep my focus and testify."

Ethan knew there was more to it. Brett had sidestepped the question about the money a couple of times now. "We're not going to let anything happen to you. The plan is still the same, and now there's a bonus. Because we know we can trust Kelly. So we stick together and get you to that courthouse to testify."

"I could bring in help. Local cops I know are solid." Kelly worked her mouth back and forth as she thought. "I hope they are, anyway.

I'm going crazy suspecting everyone is working with the O'Callaghans. But he doesn't even have to be behind this."

"Money makes people do all kinds of things they wouldn't otherwise," Ethan said. "That's all anyone cares about, and who knows what lengths they'll go to in order to find out where it is."

"First we have to figure out who even knows the answer to that question."

They both looked at Brett.

"Steer clear of the money. All of it. You step into that and you'll get caught in the cross fire."

"We already did," Ethan said. "You won't tell us what's going on. What are we supposed to think?"

"You're supposed to trust me."

Ethan stared at his brother. "I wish I did."

FOURTEEN

Kelly strode out into the hall and nearly collided with the officer at the door. "Hey, Mills."

He nodded, looking crisp in his uniform. "Wayne."

Her prayer was that she could trust the men and women she worked with, even with everything going on. Over the last two years, she'd built relationships and established mutual respect.

She thought she'd been doing that with the chief this whole time. Now it turned out he and her father had lied to her. That the O'Callaghans had killed her mother.

Her dad was right. If she'd known, this whole situation would've been entirely different.

"Hey."

She turned and saw Ethan. Kelly's eyes filled with tears. He started to say something, but she held up a hand. "Hang on." To the cop, she said, "Mills? No one goes in this room without a valid hospital ID, okay?"

He nodded.

"Thank you." She figured he thought the emotion was about needing to save the life of the witness and the threat at hand. That was fine. But all she could think about was her mother.

"Let's find somewhere quiet."

Kelly nodded. Ethan led her to an alcove with a bench seat, and they sat beside each other. It seemed so natural to lean against his strength. "I'm glad Brett is all right."

They'd found his brother, and he was alive.

If they could make sure both were protected, things would be fine for Ethan and Brett.

"But are you?"

Kelly shook her head. She didn't lift her temple from his shoulder. There was nothing on her face she wanted him to see. Not one ounce of the betrayal, the hurt or the grief.

She felt the tears roll from the corner of her eyes onto his T-shirt. She lifted her head then and swiped them away. "Sorry."

"You have nothing to be sorry for." Ethan put his arm around her and tugged her close. "Do you think he's telling the truth about your mother? Not that I believe he's lying, but it seemed like you didn't know what happened to her."

"I know what I was told. Apparently that hasn't been anything actually true." Kelly shook her head. "I feel like I know nothing about my life, or what's going on here."

She let out a long sigh. To think others had some idea of her life that she didn't, or the fact that she'd needed protecting for the last two years, was like a bad dream. He squeezed her shoulders. Even though he said nothing, she felt what she needed to hear from him in his touch and the reassurance there.

"I need to find out what really happened to her," Kelly said. "This is unbelievable. I can't even believe she was murdered, and no one told me. Not even when I became a cop."

"How old were you when she died?" His voice remained calm. Soft, and steady.

"Twelve. My dad told me she was mugged. He never said anything about his work as a detective, never even told me there was a possibility that it was anything other than that Mom was just in the wrong place at the wrong time."

She squeezed her eyes shut. Kelly needed to call her dad, or she was never going to get the truth. Not that she doubted Brett, but this was pretty far out of left field. How was she supposed to believe it when it made no sense?

But only because she'd been lied to this whole time and believed all of it.

"First the chief, now my dad." She shook her head.

"Talk it out with me."

"They've been conspiring behind my back. It's like they don't think I can handle the truth, or if they tell me I'll go off half-cocked and get into trouble. They don't trust me to be rational." She gritted her teeth. "All this time trying to prove myself, and it's like I've gone backward not forward."

All of it swirled in her mind until she wanted to tear her hair out. "And do you want to know what the worst part is?"

"What?"

"I hate people who wallow, all self-absorbed. I'm not going to do that. I won't."

His lips twitched, and she slapped his knee. "Sorry."

She shook her head. "I needed the distraction. Turns out you're a pretty good one."

"I shouldn't smile, but you're incredibly cute."

Kelly didn't even know what to say about that. She was a grown woman. Cute? She should be classy and beautiful, not exhausted and probably looking like she'd been dragged through the woods.

She blew out a long breath.

"Everything will be okay, because God is in control of it. He's never surprised, even when we are. And he knows what we're facing."

"You just remembered all that, like it was right there?"

"Things are coming back," he said. "It's getting clearer, and stuff that's ingrained in me. Like the truth that He holds me in His hands—and He always has? That's been there as long as I can remember. Even if Brett didn't believe it, I needed to. Because I needed Him."

Kelly closed her eyes and nodded. She thought over what he'd said, willing to admit that she might not have ever thought about it in terms of her *needing* God. Or that she was enough He might need her either. She'd been trying to be that way, that was for sure.

And where did all that striving get her? Two steps back at the first knockdown.

Kelly shifted on the seat and realized her phone was still in her back pocket. She slid it out and dialed her dad's number. Ethan sat beside her while she listened to it ring.

When it was clear he wasn't going to pick up, she said, "I need to find my dad."

"Do you think he's in danger? If he knows where the money is, the O'Callaghans could come after him."

She nodded. "Maybe that's why he told me to watch my back and not to contact him."

Could he really have the money?

"Would Brett know about it if your dad did have it or knew where it was?"

She shrugged. "Maybe. Do you think you can get him to talk? He seemed pretty adamant about us leaving that whole thing alone."

"Maybe, but when he's stubborn there's usually nothing anyone can do." Ethan shifted his mouth, then scratched at the stubble on his jaw.

"Protecting him so he can testify serves a purpose. But it also leaves vulnerable everyone the O'Callaghans are going to mow down in their quest to find that money." She thought of her dad being caught in that. Or the target.

"So how do we do both?"

Kelly frowned. "We'd need help. People we can trust without question, like feds who've had nothing to do with this case so far. They have to have no stake in this. The FBI could take Brett to court to testify if we explain this is a special circumstance."

"But as soon as they discover there's two million at stake, any one of them could be turned. Some people would burn everything for the chance at that kind of payday."

She had to agree. "It's a risk, but I doubt we can do all this ourselves."

He nodded. "What do you want to do?"

Kelly stood. "We need Nico."

She also needed to talk to her chief, find her dad, stop a bunch of people trying to get that missing money and get Brett to court so he could testify.

But none of that would happen without her K-9 by her side.

Kelly pulled the car up outside the police department, two buildings with a kind of quad between them, in the middle of town.

Kelly threw the car in Park and muttered, "What is he doing?"

Ethan spotted the man on the grassy area between buildings. "Is that your chief?"

She shoved open her door. He did the same, following as she trotted after her boss who held on to one end of Nico's leash. At the other end, the dog lay down, not looking like she intended to go anywhere.

"Sir?"

"Wayne." If Filburn realized he'd been caught doing something he certainly shouldn't be—like trying to steal her dog—he didn't betray that.

Ethan wondered if that meant the guy was simply good at hiding things. His heart hurt for Kelly. She'd been through so much, discovering her dad and boss had lied to her. Learning her mother had been murdered by O'Callaghan. That Brett knew more about her than she did.

That much deception couldn't possibly keep a person safe. It only kept them in the dark. Like trying to fight hand-to-hand with a blindfold on, something he knew from training experience was difficult.

He hated that she was dealing with this, but the fact she'd let him come with him meant something. They'd driven by her house, and she'd loaned him a pistol from her personal safe. She trusted him.

That may very well turn out to mean him seeing the truth about her boss when maybe she couldn't—or didn't want to.

"What's going on, sir?" At the sound of her voice, Nico perked up. The dog looked to Kelly, regardless of who held the leash. Kelly held up a hand so the dog knew to stay put while her tail wagged at the sight of her handler and partner.

She hadn't been happy before, but Nico was happy now.

"Oh, just helping Nico get some exercise."

"With all due respect, Chief, that's my job. And it's why I'm here."

The chief glanced between her and Ethan. "With company." He pinned Ethan with a steady stare. "How is your brother? I didn't get the chance to ask at the hospital."

"Stable, thank you. He was pretty beaten-up, but he should have no problem testifying against Michael O'Callaghan. And everyone who works with him." Ethan held his gaze right back, because if the chief had anything to do with that crime family, he wasn't going to get away with deceiving everyone.

"Good." The chief nodded. "That's good."

Kelly walked to him and held her hand out. "The lead, please."

He handed it to her while Ethan wondered why she called it that, not a leash. Maybe it was a professional dog handler thing.

"Thank you."

Kelly came back over to him, leaving Nico enough slack. She took up her spot beside Ethan. Solidarity against her boss.

The guy didn't miss that move. "Where are you headed next?"

"Because you think we're going to go after that money?" Kelly shook her head. "You already know I don't care about stealing just to get a payday."

"Me either," Ethan said. "For the record."

The chief just frowned. "So you're teaming up, even though bringing along a civilian is hardly procedure. Going rogue then, is it?"

"Like taking my dog from her kennel?"

Ethan gathered that wasn't an everyday occurrence. "What do you *really* need Nico for?"

The chief shook his head. "Is this an interrogation? Too bad you're not a cop, Mr. Harrigan. I happen to be the chief of police."

"That doesn't make you above the law, sir." Kelly lifted her chin. "Just because you and my father bleed blue doesn't mean you get to withhold information. Or subvert the cause of true justice."

"I know that." The words exploded from the guy, and his body tensed. His face reddened. "We're the ones who taught *you* that."

"I know," Kelly said. "That's why it's so much worse that you lied to me."

The police had a marshal in custody. Maybe the chief had found out something from him. Ethan didn't like questions he had no answers to—especially when he should know but couldn't remember. He wanted answers, like a reporter who refused to quit.

The chief's face hardened.

"Where is my father?" Kelly asked.

"I knew you'd go after your dad."

"Someone has to. If he's got anything to do with this missing money, he's in serious danger."

And Ethan got to protect her while she did what she needed to do.

For some reason that made him feel more like himself than he had in a long time.

He sucked in a breath.

"You okay, Ethan?" Kelly didn't turn, but the question was directed at him.

"I'm good. Just…remembering more things."

"Good." She paused. "Chief? Where's my dad?"

The older man stared at her. Ethan didn't like it, or the lack of answers, so he asked, "Did the O'Callaghans really have Mrs. Wayne killed?" After a slight pause, he added, "I think you owe Kelly that much."

He'd rather she have the complete truth, not what they decided to tell her at any given time. Ethan was proud of his brother for being honest. She'd been in danger. Brett had done the right thing by keeping her safe, as far as he was concerned.

Except if they'd both testified, Ethan could've met her in witness protection at some point in the last two years, when they prepped for the trial. For all he knew they could be married by now.

Another sharp inhale from him brought Kelly's attention around.

Ethan waved her off. "Chief, we need the truth."

And he needed to get his brain to quit making leaps. Sure, Kelly captivated him. She was strong and vulnerable. Independent and capable, and in need of backup, but not unwilling to accept help.

She was the real deal—the whole package— the kind of woman he could see himself falling in love with.

"Your father went to talk to O'Callaghan. To make a deal." The chief sucked in a breath, his jaw flexing. "He's going to trade the two million for your safety."

Kelly gasped.

Ethan couldn't believe what he was hearing. But just then his instincts flared.

Nico got up to stand on all four paws, ears pricked.

Ethan spun to look behind him and spotted an SUV speeding down the street toward them. The window rolled down, and the muzzle of an AR15 slid out.

He dived at Kelly. "Get down!"

Shots erupted. He guarded her with his body while she tugged Nico's leash toward her and screamed for the dog to crawl. Bullets hit the picnic table and the trunk of the tree. Dirt kicked up around them, but he didn't move.

Tires squealed and the SUV sped off. These guys had held true to the O'Callaghans' preferred method of solving things with a barrage of bullets.

Ethan lifted his head and let out the breath he'd been holding. "They're gone."

Kelly pushed at his chest. "So is the chief."

He rolled and sat up. She was right. Her boss was nowhere in sight.

"I saw him run off," Kelly said. "We need to find him."

FIFTEEN

The door opened and two officers ran out, guns drawn. The closest one yelled, "What happened?"

Kelly had one thing on her mind, and it wasn't the drive-by. Not when she'd seen the chief run off. "Get me Chief Filburn's jacket!"

The first officer blinked at her.

"Now!" She added, "Please." Just in case that would help.

Ethan held out his hand and she clasped his wrist. He hauled her to her feet.

"Thanks." She touched her forehead and felt Nico move beside her leg. Between Ethan and her K-9 partner, she should be fine. Or protected at least. So why did she feel like everything that was supposed to have been her foundation had fallen out from under her?

"Here." The officer held out the coat.

"I need to find him, so thanks." She gave Nico the scent command, and the dog snapped to alert. Nico didn't seem fazed by the gunshots. Meanwhile, Kelly's hands still shook. "Good girl."

Nico was ready to get to work.

Kelly got a good grasp on the lead and said, "Nico, find."

She turned in a circle, sniffed the ground, and immediately raced in the direction the chief had gone just a few moments ago.

Kelly jogged behind her. Ethan kept pace, and they raced across the grass between the buildings to the parking lot. Her heart sank at the idea he might've jumped in his vehicle and sped away. All of it would be on surveillance if he had. This could be a nothing search that frustrated Nico and set Kelly back.

Still, they had to try and find him. Because what kind of police chief ran off after a shooting? After they'd been hit by an AR15 attack in a driveway on what was practically the front lawn of the police department.

And then he leaves?

She was doing the same thing right now, but there was no time to explain to the other cops why it was so important. They were likely as in the dark as she was about their chief's true motives. And what he'd been up to this whole time.

Nico crossed the parking lot and passed the chief's car emblazoned with the department decal and his name on the driver's side door. If he wanted to go unnoticed that wasn't the vehicle he would use. So where had he gone?

The dog led her to the far side of the lot onto the sidewalk where she headed north up the street.

A house? A car parked on the street where the chief could quickly make an escape?

This part of their surroundings wasn't covered by PD surveillance. If he'd left from over here they wouldn't have any way of getting an image of the car or the license plate. Without knocking on doors and praying a neighbor had seen enough they'd be able to track it, they would have nothing.

Nico stepped off the sidewalk and sniffed the grass between the sidewalk and the curb.

"Car."

The dog turned and sat down.

Kelly groaned. "The trail ends here. The chief got in a car."

She congratulated Nico until her dog's tail wagged so hard she was in danger of falling over.

Ethan ran a hand down his face. He might be gorgeous, but he didn't look like he had as much energy as he should. That too-pale face seemed more like he should sit down. Or take a nap.

The cop behind him shook his head. "What's going on?"

"Honestly? I have no idea. All I've got right now is more questions than answers."

Nico wandered to the bushes on the other side of the sidewalk.

Kelly said, "I want to talk to the marshal the chief brought in. He threatened the witness and his brother, and the chief booked him." Hours ago now, and she hadn't heard anything since.

Because the chief had no intention of questioning the guy, or because he didn't want to tell her what she might need to know?

Kelly blew out a breath and felt Nico tug on the lead.

The officer shook his head. "The chief didn't bring anyone in. Certainly not a marshal. We don't have a fed in holding, but I heard there's one at the hospital."

Ethan said, "There were two taken to the hospital with my brother. The first one was arrested, though. Edmonton, right?"

Kelly nodded. "Deputy Marshal Cliff Edmonton."

The cop pulled a notepad from his pocket. "I can make some calls, see who knows what. Try to track him down." He noted the marshal's name and headed back to the precinct.

Ethan said, "What do—"

Nico's pulling got too much. Kelly whirled around. "Nico—"

The dog sat.

"What did you find?" More tail wagging. Kelly rubbed her head and looked at the ground. "She found something."

Kelly lifted a cell phone from the ground and showed Ethan.

"You think the chief dropped it before he got into his car?"

She nodded. "It's his PD phone. I'm sure he's got another untraceable one if he's really involved in something he's not supposed to be." She let out a breath, hardly able to believe a man she'd trusted could have betrayed her, the police department and the people of this town so thoroughly. And for what?

Two million dollars.

"We need to get into this phone. Maybe he didn't want us to be able to track him, but there could be texts or emails we can get to before he has a chance to delete the evidence remotely."

"Let's go, then."

She frowned. "Sure you're up to it?"

"We're getting in a car, right?"

Kelly nodded. "As soon as we catch a break, we'll get some food."

"So how do we get his code?"

"We pay his wife a visit." Kelly had seen her

using the chief's phone at a PD picnic when she couldn't find hers. "After we get in it, we can hit a drive-through."

"Sounds good."

"Do you want to check on Brett?"

Ethan shook his head. "He'll be okay."

There was a slight note of guilt on his face, like he didn't quite agree with what he was saying. She knew she'd prefer to work rather than be stuck in a hospital room. "Thanks for going with me."

He nodded. "I'd rather be with you than anywhere else right now."

She loved that look on his face. Even if their relationship was going nowhere fast, she couldn't help dreaming of what could've been, if it weren't for so many things that would pull them apart. Whether either of them liked it or not.

For now, she just wanted to be content with the fact he was here. With her. Protecting her and standing by her. He could be hiding anywhere in the world right now, or with his brother, but he'd chosen her. Something no guy had ever done for her before.

The feeling was a good one.

She studied him, feeling the tug of a smile on her face. "How many times have you saved my life now?"

Ethan grinned and slung his arm around her. "Who's counting?"

She chuckled. "Come on." Reality sobered her up quickly. "We need to get going."

As they headed for her car, her phone rang. The number wasn't one saved in her contacts, but she answered it anyway. "Officer Wayne."

"This is Special Agent Taylor Barnes from the FBI. I need to speak with you about Brett Harrigan."

Ethan drove while Kelly spoke on the phone most of the way to the chief's house. Her car's GPS indicated there was half a mile to go when she hung up and he could finally say, "What was the call about?"

"Have you ever met Taylor Barnes?"

Ethan wondered for a split second if this was a test. "A blonde woman comes to mind. But I have no idea who she is."

"She's FBI. Apparently your brother knew her a few years ago. He called her from the hospital, and she's on her way. Her plane will land in thirty minutes, and she's heading straight to the hospital. She's taking over his protection detail. She'll get him to the courthouse in time to testify, and we don't have to worry about him."

"Why does that make me feel like I just got released from prison, and at the same time it's like walking into a market square knowing I've got sniper crosshairs on my back?"

Kelly shifted in her seat. "There's a lot there."

"But we don't have time to unpack it. We're here." Whether he liked it or not, there was no opportunity to get to know each other when so much was going on. He could say that he very much wanted to stick around long enough to see what could be with him and Kelly.

If he'd been cut loose from the Marshals Service and the feds didn't care about him, he needed protection.

Would Kelly volunteer to watch his back while he gladly watched hers?

Ethan didn't like the idea the O'Callaghans could snatch him and use his life to get Brett to keep from testifying. He'd had that conversation with his brother already, knowing his one life wasn't worth more than all the ones that evil family had destroyed. Justice was more important than him having a future.

Brett would do the right thing if it came down to it.

"Let's go." Ethan grasped the door handle.

Kelly stayed him with a hand on his arm. "I do want to talk about you."

He nodded. "I'm glad Brett is safe. We'll either figure out the rest of it, or it's going to resolve itself."

"I still want to talk."

He felt his lips curl up. "Me too." He hesitated. "Will you tell me about your mom?"

"Yeah, I'd like that."

Ethan realized how close they were, sitting in the front seats of her car, leaning in. He closed the small gap a tiny amount more and saw her eyes widen a fraction.

Did she want him to kiss her?

He could list the reasons it was a bad idea, but when would they get another chance? He didn't like regret, and if he didn't take a chance on what he saw in her eyes, he'd live the rest of his life wondering what might've been.

"We should get inside."

Ethan turned away. "Sure."

"It's not because—"

He didn't want her pity, wrapped up in what was going to be a flimsy explanation.

"It's fine." Ethan pushed out the door.

He walked fast to the house, even though she was the one who had the phone. Kelly met him at the front door, where she knocked.

She was the cop. He was a federally protected witness and not even the one testifying. Just the twin brother along for the ride, at risk for doing nothing. Not that being the one in danger was the problem.

The door opened before he could dwell on

his hang-ups about Brett and his former career as a marine. How his life after the military had been cut short in the sense he didn't want to serve after that last disastrous mission. He was a teacher now, because he'd had to choose a career in WITSEC, and that was that. No point wishing for what couldn't be, or never would be again.

Kelly introduced herself to the chief's wife and motioned toward him. He couldn't hear most of what she said for all the white noise in his head.

The chief's wife invited them in, and Kelly shot him a look like, *Get it together.*

He stepped in after her and tried to do that. Except for the fact she clearly didn't see him the way he saw her. And why would she? He was a guy who couldn't handle not being the hero anymore. He was deadweight. Leverage.

And that was on a good day.

Ethan sighed.

Both women turned to him. He realized that had been a little loud. "I'm sorry. Please continue."

"As I was saying," Kelly said, using a pointed tone. "We need the chief's passcode for his phone. It's very important."

Ethan did need to get it together. He could figure himself out later, and not in the middle of whatever all this was. Taking down O'Callaghan was bigger than him, just like Kelly finding the truth of what happened to her mom.

If it was him, he'd stop at nothing to know. He was proud of her for holding it together. She was doing better than him.

The chief's wife was a round woman wearing leggings and an oversize sweater that looked brand-new. Her smartwatch slid down her forearm as she lifted a hand to brush back perfectly styled hair. She didn't touch her face, a good thing as she'd have rubbed off the makeup layered on there.

She gave a dainty sniff. "So you know?"

"What is it you think I know?" Kelly asked.

"The money." The chief's wife shrugged a shoulder. "It's practically gone now, spent. I have no idea how we'll survive the next quarter. We're going to have to sell our vacation house."

Kelly shifted in her seat.

She continued, "You didn't realize a cop probably shouldn't be renting you a farmhouse for half the going rate, right? It's because we own the place outright. Just like this one. And the one in Aspen."

"I figured he was doing me a favor as his new hire." Now Kelly knew her dad and the chief were old friends. She was probably rethinking everything about her life. And would be for some time to come.

As opposed to Ethan, who'd never have cause to do that because nothing would ever be the same. And with a fake identity, it wasn't as though he could do anything that meant something. His life had to be under the radar.

Ethan squeezed the bridge of his nose.

Now he had so much of his memory back he couldn't help wondering how he'd had all this resentment, or discontentment, bottled up in him for the past two years—and even before that.

Brett probably knew, but that didn't mean they'd talked about it. His brother was busy with his landscaping job. Things just were what they were. Neither of them had been happy in jobs that had nothing to do with what they did before WITSEC.

It was the rules. And if they followed them, they were supposed to be safe.

The chief's wife laughed at Kelly's expense.

"Just give me the code. That's all I need," Kelly said. "Or, I can take you to the station and you can answer all kinds of questions while we ask the judge for a warrant for your arrest."

The chief's wife relaxed back in her chair. "You can't compel me to testify against my husband."

"As far as I'm concerned, you're a coconspirator."

The chief's wife started to bluster.

"Give me the code, and I'll leave now."

She didn't like it, given the sneer on her face, but she handed the phone back a second later. "Get out of my house."

They strode quickly back to the car while Kelly swiped through the phone. "He's been communicating with someone. 'He's coming to you.' Do you think he means my dad? And why would the chief tell me my dad has the money when he's spent it all?"

"Maybe your dad has no idea the chief took it." Ethan winced. "Or they were in cahoots and split it."

Kelly sighed over the roof of the car. "Let's go back to the hospital. Check everything is okay with Brett. We can run by my dad's house on the way, just in case."

Ethan climbed in. Nico leaned forward for a sniff, so he scratched under her chin.

Two miles west of the chief's house, he spotted the same black SUV in his rearview. The one that had shot at them. "We're being followed."

SIXTEEN

Kelly couldn't worry about a tail when she wasn't driving. "I need to get as much as I can from this phone before something else happens and our lives are turned upside down."

"I'll keep an eye on them. Why don't you get rid of the passcode altogether?"

She knew Ethan was as frustrated as her. They could hardly help each other right now in the middle of all of this. It seemed like every time they did anything, the situation got worse. The only saving grace was that Brett was fine.

The fed he'd called sounded competent when Kelly had been on the phone with her. Taylor Barnes promised to keep him safe. It wasn't foolproof, but Kelly heard something in her tone that convinced her the woman might read Brett the riot act for putting himself in danger when she got to him.

She said, "Do you know who it is behind us?"

"Same people who shot at us earlier." His

voice sounded tight. "The front bumper is messed up, like they sideswiped someone already today."

Kelly gritted her teeth, navigated into the chief's emails and checked the drafts folder. At first glance it didn't seem to contain anything useful—or incriminating. She found one of those encrypted messaging apps in his menu, not on the home page.

It was full of conversations.

She tapped the most recent one and scanned down the chat. There were pictures. Kelly reached out and grabbed Ethan's elbow, trying to find something to keep her from spinning out uncontrollably.

"What is it?"

She let go, not wanting to hinder his driving if he had to switch to defensive in an attempt to get them away from whoever was following them. "He was talking to someone. A black-market buyer." Kelly took a breath and tried to get the words out. "He's going to *sell* Nico."

"What?" His hands jerked the wheel, but he caught himself.

"Fifty thousand. At five o'clock today he was going to meet a guy out by the old cement plant and *sell him* my dog."

"That's why he was trying to take Nico from the police station."

Kelly gasped. "And she's smart, so she wasn't going anywhere with him. She probably smelled how nervous he was." Her dog was smarter than her chief.

She fisted her free hand on her knee. "How could he do this to me?"

Ethan put his hand over hers. "He didn't take her. You didn't let him, and neither did she."

He probably felt similarly over the threat of losing his brother. The way she did about what her father was up to right now.

She bit her lip and went back to the phone. "There are messages between him and someone he calls 'Ed.' You think that's Deputy Marshal Edmonton?"

Ethan shrugged.

"Maybe they were working together. Maybe the chief killed him instead of bringing him to the station." Kelly looked for her dad's number on the chief's phone and read down their texts. "My dad told the chief he was going to see *him*. Which probably means O'Callaghan. But it doesn't say why."

"The chief's wife thinks they had the money. So it can't be to pay the guy to leave you alone. Though it might be true that that's where your dad is going."

"I'd like to think my dad would never do something like steal money, but can I know for sure?" Kelly felt like she knew nothing about the people around her. "My dad wouldn't try to make a deal with the son. Even if it was his father who had my mother killed to get him to back off, the son is supposedly new blood and doesn't care about the old guard. So why would he make a deal with my dad?"

Ethan asked, "What about the money?"

"The chief could've just told his wife they had the money and been stringing her along all this time, living lavish so she believed she was rich and making cash on the side." Like trying to sell her dog.

He squeezed her hand again. "No one will get Nico."

"Not without me, anyway."

Ethan changed lanes. He'd navigated his way back to the police station. But if they kept going, they'd get to the hospital. Either way, if the car behind tried to run them off the road there was nowhere deserted to do it. Someone would see.

She could call in police backup. Or get a road-block set up.

The chief might be lying to everyone, but the men and women she worked with were still honorable. Good cops. Assuming they weren't also liars.

Kelly said, "Keep going on this street. I don't

want to put the lights and sirens on and scare them off, but don't stop for anything."

She used her phone to call dispatch and set up a roadblock.

It would take a few minutes, but there were two units in the area. She had them park a mile and a half up to block off the road and clear the area of traffic.

"Sounds like this might get interesting."

Kelly said, "It's past time we turned the tables on these people. I'm sick of being on the losing team."

She went back to the phone, assimilating all the information she had found. "The chief has his hand in so many things it's like untangling a web. I have no idea what will come loose if I tug on one thing. Or will the mess get so knotted I'll never get it unraveled?"

She powered off the phone, since she'd removed all the security. Techs at the PD—or with the FBI—needed to go through it, find the chief and arrest him for his involvement.

The money was a nonissue if it really had been spent. And how did they know if it hadn't? Despite what the chief's wife believed, it wasn't likely anyone would admit to ripping off the O'Callaghans.

Finding her dad was personal. She might very well need to save him from himself.

Brett was being protected by the FBI agent who apparently knew him.

She had to find the truth, for her own sake. People here in town needed to know the truth about the chief.

But if Brett testified, it would all be worth it. That, and the fact this whole disaster meant she'd been able to meet Ethan.

Kelly spotted the roadblock up ahead. "Get some distance between them and us. When you get close, pull to the side of the road so you're out of the line of fire."

"Got it."

"And for the record, I wanted you to kiss me."

Ethan glanced at her quickly, then back at the road. "Didn't seem like it."

"Sometimes it's all in the timing."

Unfortunately for them, there wasn't much left.

This would be over soon.

Ethan spotted the two police cars parked across the road, one slightly closer than the other so someone running could weave between them.

No one in a car could get past without plowing through and causing a significant accident.

He pulled to the side out of the way so they could join the stand against the SUV now a quarter mile behind them. Ethan checked where the other vehicle was and saw it closing in fast—probably prepared to ram right through the roadblock.

Ethan jumped out and pulled the gun Kelly had given him. She did the same on the other side, calling out for Nico to stay down.

The cops reacted, hunkered down behind their cars with their weapons ready. Ethan saw more than one point in his direction. *Right.* He wasn't a cop.

Kelly called out, "He's good! He's with me!" She waved him to the side of the street. "Stay out of the way. I don't want anything to happen to you."

When he started to object, she held up a hand. "There's no time. And I'm *not* losing you after all the effort I've put into keeping you alive."

He nearly smiled at that. Nearly.

She was right about there being no time. Two seconds after he ducked behind Kelly's car, with Nico's nose pressed to the window above him, the SUV screeched to a halt in front of the cop cars.

His body went cold. "They've got an AR15!"

The cops ducked down. Except Kelly.

The side window rolled open and the weapon came out, already being fired by the passenger. She squeezed off two shots and the AR15 fell to the pavement.

The passenger cried out in pain.

One of the others fired at the cops on the driver's side. The cop hunkered down, and his partner exchanged fire with them. When the man switched up his aim, the cops traded off, keeping each other safe from dangerous men intent on murdering them.

The cop scored a direct hit.

Kelly came out from behind one cop car. Two officers did the same. They opened the doors and pulled out the driver and two guys from the back. One pulled a gun, about to shoot.

Ethan used Kelly's gun and squeezed off a round. The man fell to the ground.

She spun around, surprise mixed with fear on her face. "Thank you."

He nodded.

They got the guys in cuffs, lined up against the car's hood. Ethan stowed the gun and checked Nico was all right. He couldn't imagine how it would pain Kelly if her K-9 partner was hurt. But she seemed fine. Or at least unfazed by the gun battle that had happened.

Ethan moved around the hood of the car.

One of the cops glanced over. Kelly asked, "You good?"

"Yep. You?"

The cop spoke before she could. "One of you wanna explain who this is?"

Ethan said, "It's good that you don't know, given we're not sure who we can trust. If you knew who I was that would be a bad sign."

"Does that mean you don't plan to tell me?"

"I'm under Kelly's protection." Ethan wasn't sure what else needed to be said, if anything. Given the cop's face, that could be sufficient as an explanation.

"I'll be checking with the chief."

Kelly said, "Go through your lieutenant first. I'm not sure where the chief is, or if he's tied up in something."

Ethan figured he knew what the chief was tied up in. But given she might not want to jump to conclusions without solid evidence she might just be covering herself from the issue of making an accusation without credence to it. Then again, it could also be construed that she was determined to save the chief's reputation if she could. Given what the chief might be up to he wasn't sure it was a good idea.

She turned back to O'Callaghan's guys. "You're not going to stop the trial. You're all under arrest." She read them their rights.

The guy who'd shot the AR15 needed medical attention, so they called him an ambulance. He scoffed at her. "As if O'Callaghan cares about the patsy. That whole trial is nothing but a sham."

Ethan frowned. What did that mean?

"Because all he wants is his money?" She folded her arms. "Yeah, I know about that."

Realization flashed in the guy's eyes. He wanted that money.

"I'm guessing the feds seized all the family assets," Ethan said. "That two million is probably all O'Callaghan has left."

Kelly spun around. "That's it! That's why they want the money. Why O'Callaghan wants Brett so bad, or was the plane crash a diversion, or…" Her voice trailed off, and she let out a frustrated sound.

The expression on her face was exceedingly cute. She didn't know as much as she'd thought. Except she could be sure about his intentions toward her. That wasn't something she needed to be confused about, given he'd tried to kiss her.

Now he knew she'd wanted to kiss him back. But for the terrible timing of whatever this was between them, it made him feel better—kind of.

She spun back to the men in cuffs. "You're all done, so I guess it doesn't matter. You won't get the money. O'Callaghan will go down."

The man closest to her lifted his chin. "Guess you've got nothing to worry about."

A group of people had gathered on the sidewalk to watch, and a couple had their phones out recording this entire exchange. He'd been in witness protection long enough he didn't like having his photo taken, so Ethan ducked into the car and sat with his back to the cameras.

Nico sniffed at the grate between the front seats and her area.

"Hi, dog." He scratched her chin as best he could through the grate and watched Kelly usher the cuffed men to the police cars. More arrived, which was good as this whole scene would need to be cleaned up and everything put to rights before traffic could flow.

He'd never thought about all that went into being a cop.

When she got back in the car he said, "You're good at police work."

"Like your brother."

Ethan shrugged. "It's who you are. With Brett, it's a role he plays. Just a job. Maybe that's not completely fair, but it's true in many ways."

"How about you?" She pulled out.

"I don't know what I am. Having a new identity and picking a new career didn't do any favors. I guess I'm still figuring it out."

He pushed away all those thoughts. Who cared about the long term? He was only interested in being here with Kelly.

She drove this time and pulled into the drive of a house a few blocks away minutes later. Single story with a huge porch. Her dad's house.

Adrenaline still rolled through him from that gunfight. He didn't know what to do with the feeling.

Ethan frowned. "The front door is open."

Kelly climbed out, and they both pulled their guns. She got Nico from the back and headed in first. "I've got blood."

Ethan checked the street just in case, not wanting to be ambushed from behind. Then he stepped inside. "Do you see him?"

He spotted an overturned lamp and blood on the corner of the coffee table.

He said, "Is this from before, with Franko?"

She shook her head, her face pale.

They needed to check the whole house, make sure he wasn't lying somewhere unable to call for help.

She whispered, "What happened to him?"

SEVENTEEN

Kelly had to snap herself out of this. Her dad wasn't here…but she also hadn't checked the whole house. Or cleared it.

"Can Nico follow a scent, try to track him?"

Kelly shook her head. "His scent is all over this place, and fresh. There is no way for her to discern what happened and where he went in all that confusion of overlapping scents. She'd have to sort through it all."

"That makes sense." Ethan studied the entryway.

"Go through to the kitchen and check the backyard."

"On it."

Most guys didn't like a woman ordering them around. She was glad Ethan didn't object, especially considering the circumstances. Which was likely the reason why he moved quickly to do as she'd asked…ordered. Whichever. She didn't want to be alone right now.

Kelly walked with Nico through the house. The dog didn't alert, which she would if anyone was hiding in here.

When she emerged from the bathroom back into the bedroom, Nico trotted to the bed and hopped up to lie down.

Kelly's brows rose, even as a slash of pain hit her chest. "When you stay over here, does he let you sleep on the bed?"

Nico had only stayed with her dad a few times, like when she had a two-day court case. Or that time she'd been required to attend a federal training course.

"Everything good?"

She glanced back at Ethan, trying to figure out if she'd describe this situation as "good." Probably not. But she knew what he meant and nodded. "How about you?"

"Nothing in the house or outside. And I checked the garage. Your dad isn't here."

Kelly winced. "He effectively told me he was going dark, and I should watch my back while he's gone. But then the chief said he's trading the money for my safety to O'Callaghan. Which makes no sense."

"Except that your chief hasn't said one truthful thing since I met him, right? At least we have no idea whether he has or not since not even his wife agrees with him."

She liked the sound of "we" when he said it like that.

Kelly glanced around. "Where is he?"

"Signs of a struggle, and if it wasn't from that business with Franko then maybe he came back for some reason and someone grabbed him."

"The chief, maybe." She bit her lip. "Or any one of O'Callaghan's guys who think like the chief told us—that he has those two million dollars."

He blew out a long breath.

Kelly continued, "How could he possibly have that much money and I not notice? The chief has been living this lavish life. I figured he made money from the properties he rents out to people like me, and is paid well by the city, so he has enough for fancy vacations." She shook her head. "It never even occurred to me that he might be on the take, let alone that he stole from a crime family."

If this was a normal missing persons case she would go through this entire house looking for something that gave her an indication of why the victim had been abducted. Assuming from the scene here that was what'd happened. He'd been going dark. This made no sense.

Kelly pulled open a few drawers but found only clothes and a couple of personal items from her dad's police days. His lockbox was on the top shelf of the closet. She recognized a couple of storage boxes that her mom had put things in.

She couldn't bring herself to open those.

"I'm going to look through things in the office. Want to help?"

Ethan said, "Are you sure? Could be private."

"Given all the deception, I'm not sure privacy is the right thing just now." Kelly didn't like the idea of her dad's dirty laundry being aired, but he couldn't complain. Especially if his life was in danger.

"I'll come with you. Is Nico okay?"

Kelly looked at the dog, currently resting her head on her paws. She wandered over and unclipped the lead. "She's good."

Maybe she missed him. Despite his faults, he'd been good to Nico. Dogs were pure of heart like that. They wanted attention and affection, so they knew they were loved and appreciated. Sure, some dogs were rascals, but the ones who were mean had been taught how to be like that. By humans.

Everyone had flaws. She wasn't going to blame her dad for his.

Kelly had tried to work around her own for a long time. Or ignore them. Getting kicked off that undercover case left her with more hurt inside than she'd wanted to acknowledge. Because it meant someone believed she didn't make the cut, that she didn't measure up to their standard.

For years she'd believed Brett had been aware of a lack in her, the junior officer. As if his experience told him something about her she didn't know.

That she might not make it as a cop.

The idea of not measuring up had caused her to push hard to prove herself, and in some ways she probably would always be driven like that, even if she tried to trust her abilities and her instincts.

Ethan had seen something in her of value.

The Bible said God did—enough He had died for her.

Maybe it was time she started to see that in herself and trust it, to work from that place of already having what she needed inside her.

She stopped in the doorway of the second bedroom and looked at her dad's office.

"Did you ever live here as a kid?"

She shook her head. "We lived in Chicago. After my mom died my dad retired. Did some work there, as a private investigator. He worked for a law firm, mostly digging up dirt on cheating spouses."

"If he stole two million, I'd think he would have run rather than living here and never spending it. But could your chief have taken it?"

"He's been my dad's friend for years," Kelly said. "And he never lived in Chicago as far as I'm aware. So how would he know about the O'Callaghans?"

It made no sense that the chief was the one who ended up with the money. Unless her dad had stolen it and given it to him, but doing that made as much sense as the chief being the one behind it. Plus, it only painted a target on them. It did nothing to keep them all safe and off the O'Callaghans' radar.

And why would her dad have given the chief the money?

Had they taken the money to get back at that family *because* of her mom's murder? It could've been the only way to hit them—where it hurt. Taking the one thing they cared about.

Now someone had taken something *she* cared about. The only parent she had left.

She went to the bureau and started pulling drawers open. The bottom two turned out to be one deep drawer. Inside was a storage box that looked a lot like where case evidence would be stored.

Kelly pulled it out, flipped the lid off and groaned. She felt Ethan's hand between her shoulder blades and leaned toward him as she rifled through the files inside. The evidence bag containing a bloody shirt. Another with a knife inside, stained with dry blood.

"A murder weapon?"

Kelly winced. Her father had kept everything. He'd *stolen* it and kept it.

She found a photo of a woman she resembled enough that it made her heart ache. "This is everything from my mother's murder."

Ethan wanted to pull her close, but that would be difficult when she held a heavy box. "Can I help you with that?"

She let him take the storage box, and he set it on the desk. Her dad's office had a threadbare couch that was probably a dream to sleep on and an old metal desk. He certainly didn't live like a man who had two million stashed away.

Ethan hardly believed her dad had stolen the money. Neither could he imagine why her dad might've taken it and given it to the chief. There would be a good reason if it was true—one he wasn't privy to yet.

Kelly removed each piece of evidence and each file folder from the box almost reverently.

He set his hand on her shoulder and stood close in case she needed a literal shoulder to lean on. He wanted to be that support for her. She needed him to steady her—right now she didn't have anyone else. And for the life of him he couldn't think of any good reason why he shouldn't.

This wasn't even about some impossible relationship they'd never be able to have. It was only about helping her through this.

Her dad was gone. Her mom had been murdered.

She'd been lied to and betrayed. Two things he would never do to her. Not for any reason.

As far as he was concerned, there was no good reason her dad should have lied to her about what happened to her mom. Maybe when she'd been a child there was a reason not to give her all the graphic details. Now she was an adult? Her father should have respected her enough to bring her in on whatever he was doing with this box that seemed to be the case file. All the evidence collected. Everything the police had gathered on what happened to her mom.

Kelly flipped a file open. At the top it said AUTOPSY.

Ethan said, "May I?" He didn't want her to read that if she didn't have to. He wanted to spare her some of the pain. But not reality, the way her father had done. Cutting her out like Brett had. "I'm sorry."

She shook her head. "Turns out you're like the *only* honest person in my life. Which is really, really sad."

Ethan leaned over and kissed her forehead. "It seems like that right now, I know. But it's just because you're in the middle of it, and your dad is missing. Possibly hurt. The pain is fresh."

She handed him the file, and he heard a chime.

"That your phone?"

She frowned and pulled a cell from her jacket pocket. "It's the chief's…" Her voice trailed off.

He leaned over to look and saw a photo. "That's—"

"My dad." She blew out a tight breath. "Whoever has him wants the chief to ransom him back."

She turned the phone and showed him the photo on the screen. Her father with blood over his left eye. A gag across his mouth. Defiance in his eyes. He didn't like the situation he was in, but he also wouldn't let the fear control his reaction to being a captive.

Ethan met her gaze and saw that similar determination in Kelly's expression. "What are they asking for?"

"Two million dollars."

His stomach clenched.

"And Brett."

Ethan flinched. "They want my brother?"

She nodded. "Probably figure they'll kill those two birds with that one stone. Get the money and stop Brett from testifying at the same time."

Ethan rubbed his chest. "Why does that make me want to rush over to the hospital and see him?"

"Because you care, and he's under threat."

He cringed. "I'm sorry."

"It's okay," Kelly said. "I want to get my father back from them, but I'm not going to give them either of the things they're asking for."

"So what do we do?"

Ethan figured he could be Brett easily. They were identical twins, so it wasn't like anyone would believe it wasn't Brett. He could keep the ruse going long enough for a SWAT team of cops to bust in and save him and her dad.

He wasn't sure what he would do about faking two million dollars.

Kelly said, "We need to inform the FBI since they're the ones protecting Brett now. And kidnapping cases are their business even when it's not about another of their cases."

"You think they'd have two million we could borrow to get your dad back?"

She frowned. "They won't be able to get it fast enough, and why should we give these guys anything?"

"Because they'll kill your dad, right?" He didn't like saying it, but she had to face the risk of not doing what these people wanted. "So we make it look real. Until the FBI busts in. Or all your cop friends."

Kelly said, "We have two hours."

"Where is the meeting?"

"They're going to send instructions." Tears spilled onto her cheeks.

"They aren't going to kill him until they get what they want. And we might make it *look* like we're going to do that, but the fact is this is a rescue not a ransom drop. Right?"

She nodded.

He wanted to lean in and kiss her again. This time, not on the forehead. But he figured this wasn't the time to get distracted and think about himself—with her.

That would only end in them being even more distracted.

Her dad didn't deserve that from either of them. He might not be an innocent victim, but that didn't mean they wouldn't do everything they could to get him back.

Kelly set the chief's phone on the desk. "I'll close up here and get crime scene techs to come and collect evidence related to the kidnapping. Assuming they can differentiate between that and the previous disaster." She replaced everything in the file box and closed the lid. "This can come with me for later."

Ethan nodded.

He didn't like all the suffering she was going through. Not one bit. He grabbed the chief's phone and looked at the photo of her dad and the accompanying message. He didn't see anything new.

Kelly left the room, and he thought about everything she'd been through.

He didn't want her anywhere near these guys. Ethan was the one who should make the drop, pretending like the chief had brought him with the money to make the exchange. Turn himself over to the O'Callaghans and get her dad back.

It would be the best thing he'd done in a long time. The reason why God might have brought him to this place, Kelly's life, right at this moment.

Ethan stowed the phone in his pocket and headed for the front door before Kelly saw and managed to stop him. He'd call the FBI and get coverage. Solve this for her so she didn't have to suffer more than she already had.

He reached for the door handle.

Nico barked.

Ethan turned and saw the dog in the hall behind him.

"Leaving without telling me?" Kelly stepped into the hall after her dog. She folded her arms.

"You can give me back my gun first. And the chief's phone."

She had to understand it was for the best that he did this. He could get her dad back for her. It was the right thing for him to do, like with Brett and testifying. "Kelly—"

"I don't want to hear it." She lifted her chin. "If you don't want to help me, then go. But give me back those things."

EIGHTEEN

Kelly brought Nico in the hospital with her. Both of them had their vests on, designating who they were and their partnership. That was what she needed right now—the solidarity she had with her dog. The purity of Nico's affection for her.

The respect.

The connection they had that went so deep Nico felt the need to stop Ethan before he left her dad's house and went off on his own to do... who even knew what.

She could barely think about it without feeling the need to explode. What a waste of effort freaking out would be when every bit of energy she had needed to be focused on finding her dad and getting him back.

She prayed the meet wasn't too far of a drive, wherever it was. She didn't know that information yet, and they still had ninety minutes until she was supposed to deliver both Brett and the money she didn't have. As much as she'd feel good about handing Ethan over for a split second, what would that solve? Nothing. Whatever satisfaction she felt for a moment wasn't going to last.

"Can we at least talk about this?"

Kelly jabbed the elevator button. Nico sat beside her leg, and she reached down to stroke her head. It made her feel better for a second, longer than handing Ethan over to men who would kill him. "I need to talk to the FBI. That's how I'm going to solve this."

"We can work together."

The fact she needed him grated on her, but the reality was that he had to watch her back. If he was even willing now.

He was probably just like Brett and no matter what he would work it out so she was left behind and he got to save the day.

As if she would leave her dad's rescue to someone else.

It turned out that Ethan was no better than anyone else. Deceiving her, taking the chief's phone, and leaving her alone so he could go off and save her dad himself. Or trying it, anyway.

Why had she bothered to hope that he was different? In the end he was like Brett. Like everyone else who'd lied to her.

The elevator doors opened, and she strode out

onto the floor where Brett's room was located. FBI agents filled the hall. Each one reacted to her presence but quickly clocked her designation—and Nico's—as well as Ethan. She figured it was his resemblance to Brett that got them to stand down and let the two of them in.

"Your brother is awake." The first agent motioned to the door and told Ethan, "He's been asking about you."

Ethan didn't go right away. He turned to her.

Before he could say anything, she waved her hand and smiled. "Go ahead. I need to talk to the special agent in charge."

She strode down the hall, dismissing him. Sure it would look like she was in control, but the way her insides shook at the thought of not getting her dad back and having to bury another parent... That wasn't something she wanted to let any of these agents know she was feeling.

Kelly was a cop. Not the victim.

She walked up to an agent at the end of the hall. "I'm looking for Special Agent Barnes. Is she around?" Maybe the woman was in with Brett, and wouldn't that be spectacularly awkward?

Thankfully the agent pointed at the end of the hall. "Waiting area."

"Appreciate it." Kelly headed there.

When the chairs and vending machines came

into view, Kelly's steps faltered at what she saw. In the middle of a group of three agents was her police chief.

"Are you kidding me?" She strode to them.

The chief backed up, but two agents got between her and her boss. The female agent, Taylor Barnes, was slightly older than her, with blond hair secured into a professional bun.

"That's my boss." She tried to look around them at the chief. "Where did O'Callaghan take my father?"

The chief flinched. "What are you talking about?"

"You were going to sell my K-9. You arrested a marshal and never brought him to the station, so I figure you let him go. Then, when gunfire goes off at the station and we nearly get killed in a drive-by, you run off. Now my father has been kidnapped. What am I supposed to think but that you're working with the O'Callaghans?"

She waited a split second, then said, "Am I right?"

His face hardened. "I'm here to turn myself in. So I can testify. Things are going on that you don't—"

She held up her hand. "Please. Spare me, because I'm sick of being lied to."

Special Agent Barnes said, "He's telling the truth that he would like to testify. We're gathering the particulars now. But you said your father was kidnapped?"

She held up the phone she'd gotten back from Ethan. "This is his phone." She pointed it at the. "Which means that when O'Callaghan took my father, he figured the chief was the one who should pay the ransom." She sucked in a breath. "Guess what it is?"

No one said anything.

"Two million dollars they stole from the family, and Brett." And Ethan wanted to turn himself over to them. But what would that even solve? They would kill him. Did he really think sacrificing his life for her father's was a good idea?

Of course he would, if he cared about her so much that he didn't want to see her lose another parent.

She couldn't believe that might be true.

Who had ever cared for her like that before? It made no sense that suddenly someone would now.

The three FBI agents turned to her chief. Taylor said, "I'm assuming you'd have eventually gotten to the matter of the missing money, am I right?"

The chief gritted his teeth. "This isn't about money."

"Because you spent it all," Kelly said. "I just

can't figure out how, or why, my dad would give it to you."

"You think he's the one who took it?" The chief shook his head. "Never mind because that's not important right now. What's important is getting him back. And me testifying along with Brett. So the whole family is sent to prison."

"Is this about the uncle?" She'd heard one of the shooters mention him. Kelly turned to Taylor. "I've got someone in a cell at the precinct who might be able to corroborate this."

Taylor nodded. "Go ahead, Chief."

He slumped into a chair. "Michael inherited everything from his father. He thinks he runs the family, because that's what his uncle wants everyone to think. The truth is that after Brett Harrigan testifies against Michael, his uncle Derek will just keep running the family after he's in prison. Nothing will change."

"The feds seized all their assets," Kelly pointed out.

Taylor cringed. "Actually the uncle has no known ties to that part of the family business. On paper Derek O'Callaghan looks completely legitimate. We haven't touched anything that's his because he keeps it separate."

"I'm sure he didn't want to be fingered as part of them. And when Michael takes the fall, he'll keep it all going."

Kelly said, "Great. But how does that get my father back?"

The chief held her gaze. "I'm sorry he got pulled in. I'm sorry for...a lot of things."

She wanted to repeat her question.

"Don't underestimate Michael," the chief said. "But it's the uncle who has more to lose."

Ethan leaned forward in the chair. "You look better today."

Brett lifted his brows, asking a silent question.

Ethan shook his head. "I'm fine. I don't want to talk about it."

Brett's lips twitched. "Which is it? You feel fine, or don't want to talk about it?"

Ethan sighed.

Brett laughed, then groaned because doing that hurt. "You've got it bad for her."

"Sure, and of course she's completely oblivious to that fact. Or why I'd make any decision that involved her being in danger if I could do something that meant she wasn't. Naturally that's the worst possible decision." His head pounded so he scrubbed his hands down his face.

"Hurts?"

Ethan nodded.

"I can't believe you lost your memory." Brett's voice held an edge that sounded like anger and pain at the same time. "You didn't remember me at all?"

"I didn't even remember *me*." Ethan blew out a breath. "I had these guys chasing me, and no idea why. Then Kelly comes out of nowhere and saves me." Okay, so that wasn't exactly the way it'd happened, but tell that to his head or heart. He'd needed saving with no memory of who he was, or even his name. And there she'd come along.

Strong. Independent. Capable. Caring.

"I stand by my comment."

Ethan couldn't argue with it. He did have it bad for her, and it almost seemed like nothing he could do would convince her what he really wanted. Ethan let out a long sigh.

Forever. As impossible as it seemed, he wanted it all.

"It'll work out. Don't you always tell me God has a plan?"

"As if you were listening."

Brett said, "Maybe you should listen to your own advice."

Ethan figured it wouldn't take much to fall in love with her. He was halfway there already if he was going to be honest with himself. Was this really God's plan for him? He'd been chafing at life in witness protection. Wondering when things would get better. Looking for God to bring him something that shook everything upside down and gave him what his heart really wanted.

He'd come so close to having Kelly in his life, only to watch it slip out of his fingers. They couldn't make a simple plan work. How would they figure out a relationship with all the obstacles between them?

The door opened and she came in, as though his thinking about her had caused her to appear.

"Hey, Kelly."

Ethan turned to his brother, trying to figure out why his voice sounded like that. The guy seemed positively ecstatic. Brett asked her, "Anything new on your father?"

Ethan had explained some of what was happening to Brett, but that wasn't what his brother wanted to talk about. It seemed like he'd had enough of the case and just wanted to be brothers in his room. Ethan didn't blame him, but he didn't want Kelly to go off alone—with Nico— and save her father.

Which was likely precisely what she felt when he'd been about to leave without her. Except that meant she cared about him. The way he cared about her?

He didn't want to hope.

Kelly said, "The chief is making a deal with the feds so he can tell what he knows about the

O'Callaghans. He just told me to watch out for the uncle."

Brett frowned. "Michael is the one in charge."

"Remember when I told you I suspected his uncle Derek was involved?" she asked.

Brett shook his head. "There was no evidence of that."

"My instincts were right." Kelly lifted her chin. Nico wandered from her side and came to sniff Ethan's hands.

He petted her face and let her lick his chin. When he looked up, they were both staring at him. Ethan said, "We need to rescue your father, right?" The time was counting down until the ransom drop.

"You're not giving yourself up in exchange for him," she said.

"Agreed." Brett nodded.

Ethan sighed. "I can make my own decisions. The two of you don't need to protect me. I can do that myself."

"Without a weapon?" Kelly set her hand on her hip.

"If you don't want me without one, give me your backup gun again."

Brett grinned.

Kelly said, "The feds are going to shadow you. Neither of us will be in any danger."

"Sure. That sounds right." Ethan had been in

danger for years because of their case. "But I'm making the drop, right?"

"The feds think it will draw out my father's captor."

Ethan figured he didn't need to rub it in because they were doing his plan in the end.

"You'd better not be in danger," Brett said. "I need to testify without worrying about the two of you. So watch each other's backs. Okay?"

Kelly nodded.

Ethan said, "We will."

She looked at her watch, so he stood to let her know he was ready. Ethan hugged his brother. Neither of them said anything, but plenty was communicated between them nonetheless.

"Come on, Nico. Let's go." He strode out into the hall.

When he realized she hadn't followed he looked back. Kelly stared at him, her dog beside her. On the hospital bed, Brett grinned like this was hilarious.

Half an hour later he was ready to go. FBI agents were stationed all around, mixed with local PD that Kelly trusted. Only six, plus her and Nico. That was enough to save his life—if it came down to that.

"Good?"

He couldn't read her expression at all. She'd barely said two words to him in the car over here that weren't instructions on how to keep from getting killed—or kidnapped.

Part of him figured they'd shoot him on sight, thinking he was Brett. After they did that, if it was the plan, they'd kill Bill Wayne. If Kelly's father wasn't dead already.

"Sure. I'm good." Ethan thought the canyon between them might've been having a negative effect on his outlook. *God, I need Your help.* Only the Lord could change his attitude and the outcome of this attempt at a ransom drop.

Ethan walked across the forecourt of an abandoned car dealership holding the duffel bag that was supposedly packed with money. They'd given him a jacket, under which was a bulletproof vest. The jacket's top button had a camera in it, and a microphone, so they could see and hear everything.

The building looked empty, all glass and shadows. No movement. No people since the business went bankrupt a couple of years ago. He was supposed to wait under the streetlamp closest to the door.

They'd figured it was okay to risk him, since he wasn't Brett. He'd volunteered but they still had to sign off on it.

Ethan didn't feel great about the fact they were so comfortable putting his life on the line, but it wasn't like he'd allow anyone else to take his place. That wasn't how he operated.

Twenty minutes later he heard a shuffle behind him.

He turned and spotted Nico at a dead run, limping slightly. Ethan crouched and the dog nearly barreled into him. "Hey. Whoa. What's going on, dog?"

Nico shifted and snuffled. She backed up two steps, lowered her shoulders and barked.

"Okay."

She turned and trotted away, still limping.

Ethan wasn't going to stand around here any longer. Not after already waiting twenty minutes. He dropped the duffel of fake money and jogged after Nico.

All the way back to Kelly's car.

The driver's door was open, the dome light inside on. "Kelly?"

He looked around and didn't see anyone else. Kelly had been in the back seat when he arrived, hunkered down so anyone watching would think it was only him.

Now she was gone.

NINETEEN

Kelly shoved against the back seat of the car and tried to sit up. She didn't want to be slumped, vulnerable. He drove so fast she rolled, nearly onto the floor.

Kelly grunted. Her hands were tied together. Her cheekbone hurt where he'd punched her in the face. But there was only one thing foremost in her mind. "You kicked my dog. And violated the conditions of your bail bond."

Michael O'Callaghan gripped the wheel. "Stupid mutt deserved it."

"Excuse me?" He could not be serious. "She's purebred."

"Whatever."

He took a corner fast and she rolled into the back of the passenger seat. "Will you slow down?"

"Shoulda gagged you, but I didn't know you were gonna be so mouthy."

Kelly gritted her teeth and bit back what she

wanted to say. He'd known exactly where she was—and how was that even possible? There had to be a leak in the FBI or one of her colleagues. No one had come to her aid, but that was okay because they were focused on Ethan. She knew he'd worried he might be taken out in that parking lot, but now she knew the whole thing had been a setup.

"Did you kidnap my dad just to get to me?"

He shook his head. "Did I knock some sense out of you?"

"Why kidnap my dad and then use the ransom drop just to kidnap me instead?" The truth was that her dog happened to be far more valuable than her. Why else would the chief try to sell him to the highest bidder?

It was a good thing Nico hadn't let Michael take her as well. Kelly had commanded her to find Ethan so she could get help.

He sighed. "We're almost there. You can hold your questions until then."

As if he was the one in charge here? She refused to kowtow to that line of thinking regardless of the circumstances. In fact, she rejected it with everything inside her every chance she got.

All the energy drained from her. *God, don't let anything happen to them.*

Ethan and Nico had a team protecting them. She seemed to be in more trouble than they were. However, her tendency to do whatever it took to prove herself reared its head again, trying to convince her she could handle this.

But that wasn't true, was it?

The fear she'd felt at the idea Ethan could be in exactly this situation might be what he was feeling toward her right now.

Ethan had told her that God wasn't surprised, and He knew what she was facing. Just like her dad.

Kelly leaned against the seat and closed her eyes. *I'm sorry I thought I was the best person to be in control.* She needed Him to guide her life now that she was in over her head—and every day.

That was the only way she'd get a shot at a future with Ethan when she didn't even know how to get her dad back.

"Is my father alive?"

Michael O'Callaghan turned another corner and pulled behind a house. Into a garage.

The interior remained dark, even after the garage door rolled down. Then the door to the house opened, and her dad stood there.

Kelly tried to shove her door open, but it didn't budge.

"Hold on." Michael got out, then opened the rear door.

She slid across the seat—and into him.

"Easy."

"You think I'm going to cut you slack? You kicked my dog." She glanced at her dad, then back at Michael, not wanting to let her guard down even a fraction. "What's going on?"

Michael headed for the house. Her dad got out of the way, and he disappeared inside.

"You're working with him?"

Her dad shook his head. "It's not that simple." He pushed off the doorframe. "Let's get in, and I'll cut your hands free."

She stood alone in the garage trying to fathom how her father could possibly be working with Michael O'Callaghan. He'd been here, hours from Chicago, for years. Her dad never left town.

There was no way he worked for the family after they'd killed her mother.

Kelly spotted an axe on the wall. She could grab it between her bound hands. Do some damage while she demanded answers.

But didn't that make her exactly like them? The O'Callaghans made threats and destroyed property. They hurt people.

She stormed inside and found her father at the table. "You were kidnapped. There was blood on the wall in your house."

"Had to make it look good." He sipped from a mug.

Michael called out from the kitchen. "Coffee?"

Kelly pressed her lips together. No wonder that scene hadn't made sense.

"Sit down." Her dad cut her bonds and waved at the chair. "Have a cup."

Michael brought over two mugs, a bottle of creamer under one arm. "I didn't know how you like it, so it's black." He set them down, then offered her the bottle.

"You think I'm going to take anything from someone who abducts my father and then abducts me?" She wasn't going to repeat herself about how he'd treated her dog, but she wanted to. "What do you want?"

Michael pulled out a chair and sat. Kelly stared at him across the table, her dad to their left. He seemed like he was all right. A little banged up, maybe.

"What's going on?"

Michael fingered the handle of his mug. "I need your help."

"He couldn't fix your problem?" She motioned to her father.

"We need a sworn officer of the law to take my official statement."

"Great. It'll be all sewn up for the DA when you're arrested on two counts of kidnapping, to add to the charges you're already facing."

Her dad sighed. "Can you sit down, honey? Please?"

"You're working with this guy? When his family killed mom?" She couldn't even believe what she was seeing.

Her father winced.

Michael said, "My uncle had your mother killed. Everything the family did was all him. Including my father's death."

"I know Derek is the one who is really in charge. The chief is going to testify to it."

Michael flinched. "Filburn?"

She nodded.

"I'd guess that's not why he came to the FBI. We've suspected that he has worked for my uncle for a long time, since the beginning. Along with a marshal. But we couldn't figure out who."

She figured it was Deputy Edmonton.

"That's why I moved here," her dad said. "Why I needed you in the police department, honey." Her dad seemed earnest.

Kelly just blinked.

"So you kept everything from me about the O'Callaghans and let me go in blind to this police department, even though you suspected my boss had something to do with the family who killed Mom?" She felt the tears gather in her eyes but refused to give in to them.

"You had to be on the inside to see the truth. To know it because it was right, not because I steered you in that direction and you enacted a campaign based on what you believed. We needed evidence, and I trusted that you'd get it."

"So I've basically been undercover since I got here, only I never knew because you didn't tell." She folded her arms, missing the feel of a dog lead in her hands. "The chief will testify that it was all Derek's doing and not just Michael here, who is responsible. So the feds can take down the whole family."

"I had nothing to do with any of it," Michael said.

"That's what I figured out years ago," her father said. "When I tried to turn Michael into a confidential informant. After I found out you went in undercover, I thought you'd see too. Then Brett got you kicked off the case because he thought he was doing the right thing protecting you, and I realized your efforts were best served here. Figuring out the chief is dirty."

She stared at both of them. At least the FBI could keep an eye on Filburn if he was in their custody. She asked, "What do you want from me?"

"Take my statement," Michael said. "About all of it. Everything my uncle has ever done. I shouldn't be the one on trial. He should."

* * *

"What's going on?" Ethan glanced around at the cops and feds that had gathered.

One of the cops leaned in Kelly's driver's door and frowned. "She's gone?"

Fear moved through him like an icy breeze until his body shook, and he had to set his hand on Nico's shoulder to keep from listing over to one side. "You were only watching me?"

"That's why we were here," an FBI agent said. "We tend to look where the threat is coming from, not where it won't be."

"Mr. Harrigan—" Someone started.

Ethan didn't want to hear it. "What happened?" He was aware he was yelling. Sure, he'd come across as unhinged, but he needed someone to tell him something. "Where is she?"

Nico leaned against his leg, as if the dog was as worried as he was. At least someone else cared.

One of the FBI agents strode over to the group, tucking his phone in the inside pocket of his coat. "There was an incident at the hospital. They were getting ready to transport everyone out when the police chief tried to kill Brett Harrigan, Special Agent Barnes stepped in between, and she was stabbed. They're taking her to surgery."

Ethan turned to Kelly's vehicle. "Nico, in the car."

Thankfully the dog knew what he was talking about. She jumped over the driver's seat to sit on the passenger side. Ethan got in and closed the door.

"Mr. Harrigan!" The cop's voice was muffled.

Ethan didn't listen.

The guy banged on the window. Ethan shoved open the grate that allowed Nico to get in her compartment in the back. *"Platz."* That got the dog to lie down before.

"Mr. Harrigan!"

Ethan started the car and drove off before one of them got the bright idea of jumping in front of the car to try and stop him. He needed to get to his brother so badly his hands shook. He had to grip the wheel to keep from spinning out but remembered to buckle his seat belt.

He had charge of Nico and had no intention of taking that lightly. He would take care of her, and that meant driving safely.

Help me, Lord. He wanted to get to Brett. But he also had to figure out who had taken Kelly and why. She was the one without backup right now.

Ethan rolled the windows down because dogs liked that. Sure enough Nico moved to the passenger side, behind the front seat, where she could taste the air—or whatever dogs wanted from the wind.

"What are we going to do?" He had no idea where to start looking for Kelly.

Not to mention who'd taken her.

He'd had what he wanted for a short time, everything he thought he'd ever needed. No surprise it was nothing like he'd anticipated. Was what God had in mind ever what the believer thought it *should* be? Not as far as he could tell.

Kelly had been a gift he hadn't expected. Such a blessing he couldn't comprehend—a woman who captured him. Someone who made his life better.

Ethan let out a shuddering breath and squeezed the steering wheel. "God, where is she?"

He knew, and it was the only thing currently keeping him from spinning out completely.

Nico let out a snuffling noise.

"Yeah, I miss her too." The dog probably smelled something in the air that reminded her of Kelly. Or a piece of bacon. Who knew which it was?

Going to the hospital and seeing his brother would reassure him Brett was all right. What it wouldn't do was get Kelly back.

Nico barked.

Ethan let his foot off the brake. "What is it?"

Nico barked again.

"I have no idea what that means." He knew what he *wanted* it to mean, like he wanted God to intervene so badly. Show him which way to go.

Nico barked.

Ethan kept driving, part of him refusing to fully let go and hope.

She barked again and kept on barking. Ethan pulled over and parked. "If we're doing this, our best shot is to do it properly."

Of course, Nico heard none of that. Still barking. Until his ears rang.

Ethan took the keys and grabbed the dog's "lead" as Kelly called it. He went to the back of the car and had Nico sit while he got it clipped on.

"Okay."

She sprung from the car and sniffed the ground.

Ethan gripped the lead and wound it around his hand for good measure. "Let's go, Nico. Find Kelly. Find."

He had no idea if it worked. The dog could be going after a squirrel for all he knew. But he prayed with everything in him that she'd smelled something familiar and would lead him to the one person he wanted to see. The place he wanted to be more than anywhere else in the world.

With her.

Nico took off down the sidewalk, moving fast, but she almost seemed frustrated as she sniffed around. He had no idea, but sometimes it was like dogs conveyed their emotions through body language and mannerisms.

He didn't want to admit this might be futile.

Nico went about a quarter mile, turned around and headed back the way they'd come. Ethan's heart sank when they passed Kelly's car and Nico sniffed it. But she carried on, down the route they'd been driving. So she could find the scent she'd picked up from the car?

Another quarter mile and Nico headed down a driveway.

Ethan scanned the house, but it looked dark as far as he could tell. Maybe a dim light somewhere inside. It didn't seem as though anyone was actually in there.

Nico headed down the drive to a garage, attached with the door on the side of the house. She sniffed at the underside of the garage door and then sat.

"Okay, I know what that means," Ethan said. "I just have no idea what you found." He rubbed her head. "Good dog. Yes, you are."

Nico wagged her tail.

Ethan palmed the gun Kelly had put back in the glove box after she took it from him. "Come on."

They needed to find a back door.

He led Nico to the yard and a gate in the fence around back. He lifted up enough to reach over and unlatch the gate silently, then headed in. Nico found plenty of things to sniff, but he wasn't content to let her loose if he could lose sight of her.

Who knew what this place was?

Ethan crept to the patio and peered inside.

Kelly stood in front of a heavy wood kitchen table. Her dad had his back to Ethan, and Michael O'Callaghan sat across from her. None of them looked happy. In fact, it looked like a standoff instead of an agreement.

She wasn't happy, but she also wasn't being hurt.

Nico whined and scratched at the door.

Kelly whirled around to him, her eyes wide.

Behind her, down the hall at the front of the house, the front door exploded open, and an older man raced in. She backed up and blocked his view.

A gun went off.

Kelly screamed.

TWENTY

Michael O'Callaghan flew back from the force of the bullet. His chair tipped with him, and he fell to the kitchen floor.

Kelly managed to quiet the scream. *Think.*

Ethan and Nico were outside. She took an involuntary step back toward them because that was where she wanted to be.

Derek O'Callaghan whipped his arm around and pointed the gun at her.

She lifted both hands.

"Don't shoot her." Kelly's dad shoved his chair back and stood. "You've cost me enough already."

O'Callaghan sneered, the gun still pointed at her. "You think I care?"

"You should if you want a chance of getting away from here without the police and feds chasing you. Because guess what's going to happen if you leave the body of a cop with the guy you're trying to give the justice system as a patsy? All so you can continue doing what you've been doing for years?" Her dad scoffed. "No one will believe that."

"I guess my secret is out." Derek O'Callaghan had a deadly glint in his eye. "Only you'll be too dead to cause problems."

She heard a breathy inhale from her dad. The kind he made when he was overstressed and short of breath. *Not good.*

Kelly took over, holding O'Callaghan's attention. "It's hardly going to stop with us. Are you going to kill everyone who knows it's you behind it all?"

"If I have to."

"The feds will realize something is up when Michael is already dead, and the chief of police of this town suspiciously dies in federal protection." She watched his eyes flare. Sure, with this information she was putting others at risk. With a guy like this she needed all the help she could get.

Just not from Ethan.

Nico was one thing. The dog was a trained police K-9. Ethan was a civilian with skills and the will to do right. But allowing him to get hurt was the last thing she wanted. Even if he was currently wearing a bulletproof vest, so was she—which meant it was up to her to protect her father.

"I will take care of business like I've always done."

Kelly lifted her brows. "Like murdering your nephew?"

"Business."

She wasn't going to convince him to stand down. Kelly needed another way to resolve this situation—maybe the way Michael had intended, by getting her to take his official statement and clear his name. That wouldn't happen now if he was dead by his uncle's hand.

Kelly asked, "What if you could be cleared of all charges?" Her dad made a noise in his throat. Kelly reached back and found his hand. Squeezed it. She continued, "Michael was going to make a statement. Get it on official record with me. Clear his name."

Derek grunted. "You think I care about the police?"

"The less heat on you, the better. Right?" Kelly needed him to see some kind of reason, even if she was making things up as she went along. All the while she prayed Ethan was able to get to a phone and call for help. She didn't care who came.

Derek frowned.

"You could get away free and clear with the resources you've built up to start over."

"I'd rather kill the two of you."

Kelly's dad grabbed her arm and tugged her behind him. A burst of fear flashed through her. She looked at the patio but didn't see Ethan. Just Nico.

Kelly backed up far enough she could grab the slider handle while her dad yelled at Derek.

She tugged at the door. It started to slide open.

O'Callaghan swung his gun over and squeezed off a shot right beside her. The bullet hit the patio door, and glass shattered.

Nico rushed in, moving faster than Kelly could register what was happening.

She jumped on O'Callaghan, snarling.

Kelly shoved her dad aside and grabbed for Derek's flailing arm. She managed to get a grip on his wrist. The gun went off.

She heard her dad cry out.

Kelly gasped back a sob. Nico had a mouthful of Derek's jacket, tugging hard so he couldn't go anywhere.

O'Callaghan wouldn't loosen his grip on the gun no matter how hard Kelly pulled.

Derek slammed his head down. She turned her face, and his forehead glanced off her shoulder instead. Her legs nearly collapsed, but she stumbled and managed to catch herself.

He kicked at Nico.

Kelly punched him with her off hand, but it

didn't land well with no space and no power. She gritted her teeth and managed to keep the gun away from her and her dad at least.

She balled her fist and twisted her body.

A roar from her left cut through the rush of her own breathing in her ears. She barely turned before a gunshot exploded from the other side of the table.

Derek's body jerked. He dropped the gun on the floor and stumbled back. Michael stood with a gun of his own outstretched and pointed at his uncle.

But it was short-lived.

Michael stumbled and fell onto a chair. The gun clattered to the floor.

Derek reached for his gun on the floor.

Nico launched at him.

He yelped and jumped back, stumbling against the wall. He ran to the hallway and out the front door, leaving a smear of blood behind on the doorframe.

Nico rushed after him.

"Nico, come!"

The dog left bloody footprints on the floor as she turned so fast her back feet slid out and she came bounding over.

Kelly held up two hands. "Nico, sit!"

The dog stopped, panting. She sat. Unsurprisingly, she didn't seem bothered by the cuts on her pads from the broken door, but she'd feel the pain when the adrenaline wore off.

"Lie down." Kelly motioned with her hand, breathing hard. She turned. "Dad!"

Her shoes crunched broken glass as she crouched beside him.

"Just a graze." He lifted his hand from his shoulder, and she saw the wet redness on his shirt.

"I'll get some help." Kelly lifted her gaze to the open door where the cold night air rolled in. She sucked in a full breath and yelled, "Ethan!"

If he was hurt, she didn't know what she would do.

Instead of Ethan, uniformed cops stepped in. Weapons drawn. It didn't matter who it was, Kelly only saw the badges and their guns, and a wave of reassurance rolled over her. One might be dirty, but not all of them.

"Did you see a civilian out there?"

The first cop called for an ambulance and reported multiple victims, including an officer down. Considering her dad was a retired cop she was pleased they'd made that designation. He deserved that respect.

"That's Michael O'Callaghan." She pointed at the unconscious bleeding man across the table. He'd slumped over, but she didn't think he was dead. "My dog also needs medical treatment," she said. "And I *need* to know where that civilian is."

"That guy was with you?"

She spun to see the night shift sergeant. "Yes."

"He was running down the sidewalk when we pulled up. Don't know why, but I sent a couple of officers after him."

Kelly said, "He must have gone after O'Callaghan."

"This guy?" The cop pointed at Michael.

She shook her head and lifted out of her crouch. "The uncle, Derek. The one responsible for all of this."

Nico watched the whole situation, tongue lolling out the side of her mouth. She needed to sleep. After she got her pads checked for injury.

Kelly moved toward her and her partner got up, as though ready to work. "Not right now, dog. You're hurt."

"Need a hand?" the sergeant asked. The other officer helped her dad to a chair so he could sit, pale and bleeding but not hurt too badly.

"Yes, thank you." Kelly had to go after Ethan. He couldn't possibly be chasing down Derek O'Callaghan. Could he?

The sergeant crouched. Kelly said, "Up."

Nico looked at the officer who lifted her.

Kelly said, "Hang on one sec." And checked her pads.

She found a piece of shattered glass in her paw between her nails. She tossed it to the floor. There was a little blood. "That's better."

Nico turned her head and licked Kelly's cheek.

"Yeah, yeah." She looked at the sergeant. "I need to go after Ethan. He's under our protection."

He nodded. "Understood."

Kelly headed for the front door but heard a scrabbling behind her. She glanced back as Nico launched herself out of the sergeant's arms and landed like she had no injury.

"You'll get an infection."

Nico headed for the front door.

Kelly followed after her. "Fine, but we do this fast. As soon as we get Ethan, you're going to the vet."

Nico barked.

Ethan chased after O'Callaghan. Not just because there was nothing in him that would hunker down in the middle of a firefight.

And seeing the shooter flee the scene?

No way would he hide behind a raised planter in the backyard when he was the only one with the ability to chase down the guy immediately.

There was a reason God had, in His sovereignty, made it so that Ethan was here. With Kelly. And it could be exactly this—so that he could help her.

He kept repeating that over and over in his head. All while he reassured himself that she was all right. Her dad had only been grazed. And he raced behind Derek O'Callaghan.

The guy sprinted around a corner and crossed the street. How far away had he parked? Ethan expected the guy to jump in a vehicle any moment and try to run him over.

Behind Ethan, two cops yelled. Hopefully they knew this was about taking down the man in front of him. The guy behind all of this.

"O'Callaghan, stop!" Ethan yelled as loud as he could, so the cops knew he was on their side.

The guy reached a truck, leaned in the open window and pulled something out. He spun around with the huge weapon held in both hands.

Ethan dived for the ground as a shotgun round went off. He clapped his hands over his ears.

One of the cops screamed. The other yelled out his frustration. Ethan glanced over and saw him crouched by his partner, who was clutching his knee. The officer called on his radio for backup. "Officer down!"

The gun went off again.

The cop ducked against his downed partner.

Ethan rolled on the ground and came up against a mailbox. He scrambled by a pickup parked at the curb at a crouch and peered around the front bumper.

Derek O'Callaghan ratcheted it again. The sound echoed as though much louder than it was.

He would shoot the other cop next. Before their backup had even arrived.

Ethan burst out from behind the pickup's front bumper and sprinted for O'Callaghan. The guy raised the shotgun. A thousand thoughts went through his head. All of it coalesced into the knowledge that he'd act to save a life. In a way he knew it was the right thing, down to his bones, he knew he was built to give his life for other people.

Ethan pushed all thoughts from his mind and pumped his arms and legs like the life of someone he loved depended on him getting to the guy as fast as possible. O'Callaghan noticed him and flinched, turning as Ethan shoved the shotgun out of the way. O'Callaghan's back slammed against the truck. Ethan grabbed the guy's wrist and bent his arm back into the open door.

O'Callaghan cried out, and the shotgun started to drop. Ethan punched him in the side, but the guy barely flinched, jacked up on adrenaline and maybe something else. Whatever gave him the courage to take lives and continue destroying others just for money.

Blaming all of it on his nephew so no one ever knew he was the one behind it all. So he could continue unchecked. Profiting from evil.

O'Callaghan grabbed the shotgun. Ethan lifted his hand to punch the guy again, because he had no weapon other than himself and his will.

O'Callaghan slammed the shotgun into his head. Ethan's back crashed onto the ground, and he blinked up at a cloudy night sky trying to figure out what just happened while pain thundered through his skull.

"Ethan!" Kelly's cry rang out.

He heard a door slam, and then an engine roared.

The truck sped away in a cloud of exhaust and heat that blew across his face.

She landed on the ground beside him with a cry. "The ambulance is on its way."

Ethan shook his head. "Ouch."

"Tell me what my name is." She gasped the words.

That guy was getting away. She had to go after him. "O'Callaghan..."

"Please tell me that's not what you think my

name is." She groaned. "I hope you don't have amnesia again. Or still."

"I remember that I love you now." Ethan needed to tell her like he needed to take his next breath. "Why am I always injured? We need to go after him."

She frowned. "You need a doctor."

"Hasn't helped so far." He sat up. Everything spun, but she held his arm and he managed to keep from throwing up. "Where's Nico?"

"She needs a doctor as well. Maybe I can find one that will treat both of you, and this time you should stay there until you're completely all right." Kelly waved, and he spotted the dog waiting a few feet away.

Ethan held up his hand and she wandered over, slower than he'd have thought. "You okay?"

The dog licked his face.

Ethan smiled, but it was short-lived. "We need to catch O'Callaghan first."

She frowned. "You're not going anywhere."

Nico sat beside him and laid her head in Ethan's lap.

Kelly sighed. "You guys stay here. I'll get my car and pick you up. When the scene is secure, we'll go locate him. After that we're going to call the feds and *they* can arrest O'Callaghan."

"Is your dad okay?"

She nodded.

"And that cop over there?"

Kelly paled. "We're taking down O'Callaghan. And I'm going to pray the officer recovers quickly from that broken leg."

He nodded. "I'll do that as well while you get the car."

Kelly stared at him, looking like she wanted to say something. About what he'd said to her? Ethan didn't need her to reciprocate the feelings out of obligation.

He couldn't read her expression. She was about to speak when someone yelled, "Officer Wayne!"

And the moment was gone.

"I'll be back."

"I'm not going anywhere."

She shot him a look, then jogged away.

TWENTY-ONE

Kelly listened for the dispatcher's response through her car speakers. She could see Nico in her rearview mirror and nearly told her to lie down, but the answer came.

"Copy that, Officer Wayne. They will stay put and wait for the FBI."

"Thanks." She tapped the dash screen and the call ended.

"So he's at a motel?"

She nodded, glancing quickly at Ethan sitting beside her in the passenger seat. She was glad he and Nico were with her, but they should both get seen by a doctor before they did anything beyond getting out of this car.

Sure, they might act as if they were fine. She figured that wouldn't last forever.

She said, "The BOLO went out to everyone listening. A patrol car across town spotted the truck with the license plate you gave us and they're going to wait until we get there."

"And the FBI, right?"

"We can watch him get arrested, assuming you're not having a medical emergency."

He said nothing. She should try to figure out what that was about, but the fact was all she could think was that he had told her he loved her.

Kelly's heart squeezed in her chest at the thought of it. Ethan had become important to her in just a few days. The idea of it was jarring, considering she'd been all about Nico and her career before that. To suddenly be so drawn to a man in her life made it seem like everything had flipped upside down.

He'd told her to trust God, and she knew it was the right thing. It also seemed riskier than anything. It worked when Michael kidnapped her. She was safe, and her dad hadn't been hurt badly, even if Michael was in critical condition for his troubles.

Whether he was innocent or not, getting caught up with his family's business had nearly taken his life.

The cop having surgery on his broken leg was the one she should pray for.

It seemed so selfish to worry about herself in the midst of what was going on. For years she'd only been concerned with being the best police officer and K-9 handler she could be.

That wasn't in jeopardy even when the handsome man beside her took up so much of her head and heart.

She'd ignored relationships. Put her career first after Brett's actions had set her back several steps. If she was relying on God to direct her, she could choose to believe He'd brought Ethan into her life—regardless of the cause of the plane crash. Was it okay to see Ethan as being here at the perfect time, right when she needed someone?

She hoped it was true. Even after she'd ignored God's leading for so long.

Still, he would leave and go back to WIT-SEC before she got the chance to see what forever might look like with him. And that part of all this made her want to curl up in his arms and cry.

Kelly pulled into the motel parking lot and spotted the pickup. She found a space where she could see it, but O'Callaghan wouldn't be able to see them.

"So we just wait for them?"

The cop car was on the street, far enough away they could spot the door and the pickup, but unless O'Callaghan came outside he wouldn't see them.

"This guy shot a cop." Kelly didn't know how to explain it better than that. "If we go in and he gets away again, we could lose him for good. I'm not prepared to let that happen. Unless it becomes necessary to move in."

"That makes sense."

"You never thought about being a cop?"

Ethan shook his head. "I don't have the temperament for it. And being a high school teacher isn't much different than being deployed. It's a war zone."

She chuckled. Nico lay down in the back with a groan.

"Not really, but you know what I mean."

She couldn't take her attention from the door to the motel room where the pickup was parked, but she wanted to look at him. She needed to soak up these quiet moments so she could draw them back to memory when she was lonely and missing him.

The dispatcher had told her that the cops had seen O'Callaghan go inside. She wondered what he was doing, considering running was his best option.

Maybe he didn't know they were on to him.

Or he could be in there packing his stuff.

They'd said the FBI was a few minutes out. She needed them to get here soon. Before O'Callaghan made a run for it.

Ethan continued, "I picked teaching because it interests me, and it helped to keep my profile low aside from the local area in Sacramento. I wanted to make a difference in a new way, something different from being a marine."

She understood that. "After my mom died, my dad would take me to the precinct in Chicago before he retired. They would watch me if he had to work late. I went to all the police picnics and BBQs in the summer. They were all my aunts and uncles." She remembered a time in junior high when she had a run-in with the school bully and uniformed officers showed up at school the next day after she told the desk sergeant. "They didn't let me get away with anything, and they always looked out for me."

"And now?"

"It's all about Nico." She smiled to herself, still watching the motel room door. "Being a K-9 handler is all I want to do."

"What about this town?"

"I do like it." She grimaced. "Despite how I was lied to in order to get me here."

She wondered if he was feeling her out, trying to gauge how receptive she'd be to leaving. Even if her dad had lied to her, he was still all the family she had left. Could she really leave him?

She doubted the Marshals Service would allow her and Nico to enroll in WITSEC. Derek

O'Callaghan could present a threat to them for the rest of their lives.

Her dog was technically the property of this police department. Who knew what would happen if she asked to take Nico with her? They could be separated for good and not allowed to work together. But unless she did that, did she have a shot at a life with Ethan?

Maybe it was way too soon to take that risk.

Kelly bit her lip.

O'Callaghan walked out of the motel room with a suitcase. He lifted it and hefted it into the back of the truck.

"He's running." She shoved her door open.

If she let him go, then the man who had killed her mom would get away. Literally. With murder.

Kelly wasn't going to let that happen.

She raced across the parking lot with her gun drawn. She didn't see any weapons on him, but he could have anything hidden away.

"O'Callaghan, stop!" She closed in with her weapon raised and pointed at him. "You're under arrest."

Ethan watched her take that strong stance that seemed so familiar now. In just a short time she'd become so much a part of his world he couldn't bear to have to walk away.

Nico sniffed at the grate. He unlatched it in case she wanted to clamber into the front with him.

He smiled to himself and watched the stand-off between her and O'Callaghan. It didn't sit right that he would stay in the vehicle and let her put her life on the line. That wasn't the kind of man he was. However, this was her job, and he wasn't a cop. Far too many times already he'd inserted himself in the middle of police matters.

For Kelly? He would break all the rules.

Even though he cared about innocent lives and justice, it was still mostly about doing right by her.

Which was why he'd asked her how she liked it here, in this town. Ethan could live in a place like this. Especially if he had Kelly, and Nico and Kelly's dad. She had a home here. Ethan had a place...nowhere. He'd done what he had to and gone with his brother.

But what if he walked away from witness security and took the risk?

Put it all on the line to have a future.

It was entirely possible he would be killed within days, just to get back at Brett's agreeing to testify. Even from prison, O'Callaghan could be a threat. A serious one. If a bullet meant for him hit Kelly instead? He didn't know how he would be able to handle that.

He'd had a bad attitude the whole time he was in witness security. Ethan tried to hide it from Brett, as though that was even possible. His brother knew exactly how he felt about having his life upended, but thought he'd been doing the right thing by keeping Kelly out of it. And if she'd been with them? She wouldn't have been sent to the same location so he'd likely never have met her.

Brett's cutting her out of the case as a favor to his training officer meant this entire situation happened. For all the death, chaos and injury, he'd opt to relive the entire thing if she was what he was given at the end.

Kelly was a gift he hadn't deserved. He'd complained repeatedly to God that it wasn't fair he got dragged into a situation that had nothing to do with him. And yet, all along He had a plan Ethan hadn't bothered to look for—or ask for. God had given him so much.

Thank You.

He would live the rest of his life in gratitude for this, even if he never saw Kelly again. God had given him a gift anyway. Ethan had been surprised and delighted by her.

It had renewed his faith in the goodness of God.

Out the windshield he saw her close in on O'Callaghan. Two officers in uniform also held their guns on the guy. He should be in cuffs in moments.

Nico shifted to the left side back window. He heard the dog inhale.

She barked.

Ethan whipped around to look out the driver's window and saw a guy creeping, wearing dark clothing and carrying a weapon. He couldn't make out the guy's face.

He clambered over the seat and shoved the driver's door open.

The guy noticed him, but too late. The door hit him in the arm, and his gun went flying.

"Hey!" Ethan jumped out. His foot glanced off the edge of the seat. He cried out and used his other leg to launch at the guy.

A gun went off.

Someone screamed, but it didn't sound like Kelly.

Ethan and the guy slammed to the ground and started to wrestle. Pain lanced through his ankle, but he ignored it and let out his frustration trying to subdue this guy. He and Brett had wrestled their whole lives and still did it at the gym often. It was almost therapeutic.

Nico joined in a moment later, growling but basically just watching his back. She sounded ferocious but didn't move from her spot guarding him.

Ethan managed to pin the guy and pulled his arms back as cops did. Every breath in his lungs was hard-won. Within a few inhales he managed to get his breath back. He looked up.

Kelly stood there. "You good?"

He nodded.

"Nico, sit." Kelly motioned to the guy on the ground. "I can take care of him for you." She pulled cuffs from the back of her belt.

"O'Callaghan?" Ethan shifted to a crouch so she could cuff the guy.

Kelly said, "He pulled a weapon. One of the officers winged him, and he's getting a set of cuffs of his own."

The distant buzz in his head turned to the roar of engines. Black SUVs and police vehicles bumped the curb into the parking lot, filling it with the sound of running vehicles and the constant flash of police lights.

Ethan stood and felt Nico lean against his leg. Kelly walked the guy she had in cuffs over to the feds.

"Mr. Harrigan?"

He turned. The speaker was a young FBI agent he'd met in the last day or two. Anyone he'd met longer ago than that would be suspect in his mind. But then again, O'Callaghan was headed for the hospital and then prison. This was over.

"Sir?"

"Yeah." Ethan scrubbed a hand down his face. "What's going on?"

"I need you to come with me. It's not good for you to be out in the open."

Ethan said, "One second." Nico was loose, and he didn't think he'd be doing Kelly any favors if he left the dog to get lost, hurt or stolen. "Nico, come here."

He held the door open. "In." Ethan waved to the dog.

Nico hopped into the driver's seat. He shut the door.

The FBI agent stared at him.

"Okay, where are we headed?"

"We're going to meet up with your brother at a safe house."

Ethan didn't get any red flags off the guy, or any of the agents waiting with him. He'd known this moment would happen since he remembered who he was. Now it was time to leave and he didn't want to.

Kelly stood over with the cops and a couple of agents. They loaded the cuffed man into an SUV along with O'Callaghan.

The guy saw him. Derek O'Callaghan strained against his cuffs. "Harrigan! I'm going to kill you! Harrigan, you're dead!"

He thought Ethan was Brett? As if the feds

would bring his brother to an unsecured location with a man trying to kill him.

Kelly turned to him, and they stared at each other for a moment. He didn't want to leave. She looked at the agents around him. After a second she lifted her hand to wave.

Ethan wasn't going to let that be their goodbye.

He strode to her, right into her space. Her eyes widened a second as her mouth curled into a smile. Ethan slid his arms around her. She linked her fingers behind his neck.

He pressed his lips to hers and said every bit of what he wanted to aloud there in that single touch. They likely created a spectacle, but he didn't care. Nothing around them penetrated through the conversation of their kiss.

When he pulled back, she didn't lower her arms. Her gaze drifted over his face, and she said, "I know. I love you too."

Ethan kissed her once more. A quick lip touch. And then he left.

TWENTY-TWO

Six weeks later

Kelly unlocked her front door and let Nico in, holding the newspaper under her arm. The headline above the fold was all about how the sentence had been handed down for Derek O'Callaghan. Life in prison with no chance of parole.

Nico trotted ahead of her through the house, hit the dog door and trotted outside.

Kelly sighed. The last few weeks it seemed like everything had changed. Her father was the new interim police chief, but only until the mayor appointed a fresh face to take the position permanently. Someone younger, a local who'd grown up here that the town knew was incorruptible.

She just hoped whoever they were, they liked dogs.

O'Callaghan's whole operation had been

disbanded. Michael had testified against his uncle, along with Brett. Both of them had disappeared—probably into WITSEC—kind of like the way Ethan had after he got in that FBI vehicle. Never to be seen again.

Her dad had tried to talk to her about Ethan, but what was the point? She had a job to do here, and how would she even find him? He was gone.

Instead, she'd had her dad walk her through every bit of her mom's murder case. It had been added to the charges against Derek O'Callaghan. And the former chief. Derek himself had paid Filburn the two million, but Michael had considered it missing—hence everyone looking for it. The truth was that the former chief was paid for a job done.

Filburn had killed her mother.

Kelly stared at the contents of the fridge and tried to figure out when she'd opened it. Justice was coming for her mom. Filburn had been arrested after he'd stabbed Special Agent Barnes trying to get to Brett. Now it turned out a man she'd respected was the one who'd taken her mom from her.

The chief's wife had bought a plane ticket to Mexico. She couldn't be compelled to testify against her husband anyway, but Kelly knew the FBI had interviewed her several times. She'd spoken with Special Agent Barnes a couple of weeks ago about everything.

Taylor hadn't mentioned Brett or Ethan.

The NTSB and FBI agents had crawled all over the crash site and concluded mechanical failure was the cause of the crash. The assumption was that one of the marshals brought it down so he had a shot at the two million and a favor from Derek O'Callaghan for stopping Brett from testifying. The whole agency was reeling, several people had been fired and there was a massive investigation happening.

The body of Deputy Marshal Cliff Edmonton had been found, and the investigation into his death concluded Chief Filburn had murdered him. Most people thought Edmonton was the one who'd brought the plane down.

Nico barked from the backyard. Kelly frowned, but the blinds were closed so she couldn't see.

She should make a quick dinner to get to her off-duty assignment—the one she'd given herself.

Kelly was studying for the detective's exam.

Going through her mom's case had been heartbreaking. It had also intrigued her.

Nico barked again.

Kelly went to the door and opened it. Night had fallen, but as she opened her back door, the exterior lit up in a wash of twinkly lights. Her pergola had been strung with strands of lights she didn't own. A table in the center of her patio had been laid with a tablecloth and two place settings.

She wasn't alone.

Nico sat beside a guy with a thick beard growth and dark hair, but she recognized him. A disguise?

Beside him, her dad stood by the light switch with a huge grin.

Kelly didn't need her dad for this. "You can go now."

He tipped his head back and started laughing. He wandered to her and kissed her forehead. "Love you, honey."

Kelly sighed.

The door closed behind her and she stared at the guy who'd apparently claimed her dog. "Nico, place." Kelly pointed to the open crate she left on the patio all the time.

Nico lay down with a groan.

Ethan ascended the two steps to her patio. "Hey." He seemed nervous. She could see it in his movements and his expression.

"I thought I would never see you again." And now he was here. She barely knew what to think, let alone what to say. Dinner meant something—but he needed to say the words. The ones she'd wanted to hear since she met him.

The ones she had lost hope she would ever hear.

Ethan shook his head. "I'm sorry you believed that for even a second."

"I know you didn't have a choice."

"Except that I did." He came close and stood in front of her. He looked tired, but good. Really good. "As soon as I could, I chose to exit witness security. Because I want to be here with you."

"You'll be in danger. O'Callaghan will have you killed." She scanned his features. "Dark hair and a beard aren't going to cut it."

"I made a choice."

She started to argue, but he continued, "Before word came down that Derek O'Callaghan killed himself in prison rather than serve his sentence."

Kelly gasped.

"Brett is staying in witness protection, as is Michael. Just in case any of Derek's associates want to retaliate," he said. "But I was given clearance to leave, as long as I put certain measures in place and check in often. They're going to let Brett and I see each other once in a while if they can arrange it in a completely secure way. But they honestly don't think anyone is left with the drive to use me to find him. The risk is minimal."

"You'll hardly get to see your brother."

"We can contact each other. And honestly I don't know how much longer he'll last before he asks to get out as well. He's seriously into that FBI agent, and nothing is going to happen with him in WITSEC."

Ethan took her hands. "I wanted to be here with you. No matter the risk. I'll do everything I can to minimize it. Including taking a job with the police department as a weapons instructor."

Kelly's brows rose.

"Your dad figured it out for me."

"Seriously?" She could hardly believe this was happening.

He nodded. "I love you. So…yeah."

She couldn't help the laughter that bubbled up. "Yeah."

"Well?"

Kelly pulled his face down to hers. "I love you."

He smiled. She touched her lips to his and kissed him, sinking into everything that was Ethan Harrigan. The man she had fallen for during the worst days of her life. They would have to get to know each other in peaceful times, but that would be more enjoyable than running for their lives through the woods. She was sure of it.

When she lowered her heels back to the ground, Nico barked.

Kelly giggled. She looked at the table. "Were you planning on feeding me?"

"I figured I owed you since you kept me alive."

"We're square as far as I'm concerned." She spotted a cooler beside the table and found hot food inside.

Ethan held her chair while she sat, then took the one across from her. "We should say grace. I have a lot I'm thankful for."

She smiled, and he held her hand. "I love you, Ethan."

"I hope this is the first of many dinners." He lifted his water glass with his free hand. "To saving each other's lives. Partners for life, I hope."

Kelly lifted her glass and clinked it against his. "For life."

"And much more."

* * * * *

Dear Reader,

Thank you for going with me on this high-octane ride. I hope you had your hands and arms inside the cart at all times because what a thrill. Sometimes a book takes me by surprise, and this one did. I knew I loved Kelly and Ethan and that Nico would steal the show like all great K-9s. Their relationship had its ups and downs, but I was drawn to the truth that God is sovereign even if things don't seem right.

Often it's hard to see God's hand in the midst of pain or struggles. Hopefully this story helped you know that we can find peace in any circumstance. That even when things are confusing, God can be our refuge and help. There is always so much to be thankful for.

You can find me and my books at www.authorlisaphillips.com and see what's coming next. God bless you richly and,

Happy reading!
Lisa Phillips

Get 4 FREE REWARDS!

We'll send you 2 FREE Books plus 2 FREE Mystery Gifts.

FREE Value Over $20

Both the **Harlequin® Special Edition** and **Harlequin® Heartwarming™** series feature compelling novels filled with stories of love and strength where the bonds of friendship, family and community unite.

THE 2022 LOVE INSPIRED CHRISTMAS COLLECTION

Buy 3 and get 1 FREE!

May all that is beautiful, meaningful and brings you joy be yours this holiday season...including this fun-filled collection featuring 24 Christmas stories. From tender holiday romances to Christmas Eve suspense, this collection has it all.

YES! Please send me the **2022 LOVE INSPIRED CHRISTMAS COLLECTION** in Larger Print! This collection begins with ONE FREE book and 2 FREE gifts in the first shipment. Along with my FREE book, I'll get another 3 Larger Print books! If I do not cancel, I will continue to receive four books a month for five more months. Each shipment will contain another FREE gift. I'll pay just $23.97 U.S./$26.97 CAN., plus $1.99 U.S./$4.99 CAN. for shipping and handling per shipment.* I understand that accepting the free books and gifts places me under no obligation to buy anything. I can always return a shipment and cancel at any time. My free books and gifts are mine to keep no matter what I decide.

☐ 298 HCK 0958   ☐ 498 HCK 0958

Name (please print)

Address   Apt. #

City   State/Province   Zip/Postal Code

Mail to the Harlequin Reader Service:
IN U.S.A.: P.O. Box 1341, Buffalo, NY 14240-8531
IN CANADA: P.O. Box 603, Fort Erie, ON L2A 5X3

---

*Terms and prices subject to change without notice. Prices do not include sales taxes, which will be charged (if applicable) based on your state or country of residence. Canadian residents will be charged applicable taxes. Offer not valid in Quebec. All orders subject to approval. Credit or debit balances in a customer's account(s) may be offset by any other outstanding balance owed by or to the customer. Please allow 3 to 4 weeks for delivery. Offer available while quantities last. © 2022 Harlequin Enterprises ULC. ® and ™ are trademarks owned by Harlequin Enterprises ULC.

Your Privacy—Your information is being collected by Harlequin Enterprises ULC, operating as Harlequin Reader Service. To see how we collect and use this information visit https://corporate.harlequin.com/privacy-notice. From time to time we may also exchange your personal information with reputable third parties. If you wish to opt out of this sharing of your personal information, please visit www.readerservice.com/consumerschoice or call 1-800-873-8635. Notice to California Residents—Under California law, you have specific rights to control and access your data. For more information visit https://corporate.harlequin.com/california-privacy.

XMASL2022